Tall Rider

When Reuben Calthrop shoots an unarmed range-rider because he was bested in a horse race, he starts a chain of events that can only end one way: with spilled blood. Bart Chandler, a farm boy who is handy with a gun but no killer, sets out to avange the cold-blooded murder of his brother.

But Bart is not the first to go after Calthrop, who has cut down many who came looking for retribution. It will take a man who rides tall in the saddle to settle the score.

Is Bart Chandler that Tall Rider?

Tall Rider

Joseph John McGraw

A Black Horse Western

ROBERT HALE · LONDON

© Joseph John McGraw 2006
First published in Great Britain 2006

ISBN-10: 0-7090-7918-4
ISBN-13: 978-0-7090-7918-7

Robert Hale Limited
Clerkenwell House
Clerkenwell Green
London EC1R 0HT

Typeset by Derek Doyle & Associates, Shaw Heath.
Printed and bound in Great Britain by
Antony Rowe Limited, Wiltshire.

CONTENTS

1

MISTER REUBEN CALTHROP

When a man's been on the trail for three months pegged to a diet of beans, jerked beef, biscuit and dust, with never a taste of liquor from one week's end to the next, no one should be surprised if he feels a thirst come on when he hits town.

Not that Berry's Crossing, Kansas, was much of a town. It seemed bigger and busier than it really was. Besides the emigrants who were always passing through looking for gold out West, the town had a regular population of maybe 3–400 souls, farmers and their families almost all of them. Back of the buildings that lined the only street was always a collection of tents and wagons belonging to travellers passing through. On the street there was an Indian agency, a subscription school and a store. Also a saloon, The Prairie Dog, which was a sight for the sore eyes of any *bocarro* who had been droving the

400 or so head of horses he and his fellows had caught and broken out west and herded eastwards for fifty days across the plains, over a good half the length of the Californian trail, to sell in the States.

They were eight *bocarros* making the trip. They made camp outside Berry's Crossing, on the banks of the wide, slow, shallow Kepwejo River, first watering the horses in groups of thirty then leading them to graze in a natural enclosure on the other side. After settling the herd, the men pitched their tents, for they intended to stay put a while, to rest up the horses who needed to recover from the rigours of the harsh trail they had been on for months and put on some weight.

When they'd eaten, the eight drovers rolled out their blankets around the wagon that carried their supplies much as they'd done for the last fifty days, and slept.

Next morning, they set about making a more permanent camp. Then they drew lots for who would stay with the herd and who would get to take a first look-see around town. Four would go and four would stay put. Bart Chandler was one of the lucky ones, and drew a long straw. He took a wash in the stream, shaved the stubble off his face and sat still for a comrade to cut back his bushy, overgrown hair. Then he dusted off his sombrero, brushed his buckskins down with a branch of teazle, and gave his boots a shine. He was ready.

'C'mon, Jess,' he said to a grizzled old-timer who

had also drawn a long straw but had spent much less time on his titivating, 'time we was off.'

'No sense in hurrying, Bart,' the old man grinned. 'If we start by running and racing we'll be all wore out before we git there!'

Jesse Hayes drove the wagon and was the drovers' cook and general do-all. Known as Old Jess, he was anywhere between fifty and seventy, sturdy, a wise old bird with always a cheery word for every situation. He saddled up his chestnut mare which was probably as old as him and prodded her into a leisurely amble as he went in pursuit of Bart. He had already set off with the two other drovers who had been winners in the lottery, Eli Hook and Billy Rively, also smartly turned out for the occasion.

Berry's Crossing had just the one street. The store and the agency faced each other halfway along and The Prairie Dog stood at the end furthest from the Kepwejo river, so the *bocarros* rode right through the town. It didn't take long. The saloon was the tallest building, having a third floor which afforded a wide view of the country roundabout. Here the land was flat and dusty, and a single-track dirt trail led east towards a ridge of low hills which hung like low cloud over the distant horizon.

Talking quietly among themselves, Bart and the drovers rode slowly up the street towards The Prairie Dog and hitched their horses at the rail.

It was Saturday and not yet noon. But the saloon was open and doing business. Inside were several dozen men, a collection of farmers, cattle-drovers and hired hands. The place was full of noise and raucous laughter which faltered momentarily as the newcomers walked through the door.

'And what do we have here?' said a scoffing voice in the lull. 'My, my! Bunch of simple boys from back East, wet behind the ears and looking as if they ain't seen a man's drink in a month of Sundays. Reg'lar travelling men, I'd say.'

The three men sitting at his table laughed and nodded their heads.

The scoffer was a tall, well-built man of twenty-five or thirty with blond hair and a Mexican moustache. He was dressed in black from boots to hat with only his fair hair, the pearl-handle six-shooter in its fancy holster and a red sateen waistcoat to make a contrast. Everything about him – from his air of strut and swagger to the cronies and hangers-on who nodded their approval of everything he said or did – proclaimed that here was a man who liked having his own way.

'Wrong, mister,' grinned Jess, as he passed by heading for the bar. 'Fresh in from out West with a drove of fresh-broke horses. But you're right about not seeing a drink in a long, long time. Bartender,' he called, 'bottle of whiskey needed here and four glasses.'

The four companions sat at an empty table to wait for the bottle to arrive.

'Cain't sit there,' drawled the man in black.

'Table's reserved.'

'Don't see nuthing to says how it's reserved,' said Eli.

'You deaf, boy? There's no notice to say horse-drovers are dirt-ignorant, but that don't mean it isn't the case. Table's reserved if I say it is.'

Bart turned to react to the insult, but Jess placed a restraining hand on his arm.

'Cool heads, boys,' he said quietly. 'We don't want trouble. We come for a peaceful drink and that's what we're going to have.'

He stood up and led his companions to another table at the far end of the bar.

'That's better,' said the man in black. 'The smell of horse-wrangling was overpowering. Fit to make a man render his breakfast.'

His cronies guffawed.

The bartender appeared with the bottle and four glasses.

'Who's the dude?' asked Bart.

'Reuben Calthrop. He's not from around here. Jest passes through from time to time, usually looking for trouble. You don't want to go messing with Rube. Got a temper on him like a riled hornet. Also a very bad loser. Don't like being bested at nothing. Now that you know what you know, are you sure you still want to sit down and drink this?'

'Set 'em down right here,' said Bart. 'We come a long way for this and we're not going to wait any longer.'

11

He reached for the bottle and poured four drinks.

It was rough whiskey. It rasped on the throat and kicked like a mule, but it tasted good and was guaranteed to wash away the trail dust that collects in a man's throat.

'No hard feelings, boys,' said Calthrop across the room. 'A lot of greenhorns that pass through that door don't know one end of a horse from another. You was so spruced up we had you down for a bunch of gold-diggers with high hopes. Enjoy your drink.'

Bart and Jess and Eli and Billy relaxed and the level of whiskey in the bottle went down as they rediscovered the forgotten delights of sitting in a chair and leaning elbows on a table.

'Come from out West, you say,' Calthrop called again.

'Colorado,' said Jess.

'Easy passage?'

'So-so. Indians pretty much left us alone. Or else they was fighting each other for a change. Lost a few head, but we got off light overall.'

'What you got?'

'Nigh on four hundred fully broke ponies,' said Bart. 'You can see for yourself. They're resting up down by the river. You in the market for horse-flesh?'

'Could be, if your goods are the quality you say and the price is right.'

'Quality?' said Bart. 'Why there's any number of ponies in the herd that could run the legs off any horse in this county.'

'You don't say,' said Calthrop, a note of interest in his voice.

'I do say. Best Colorado stock and in prime condition.'

'Maybe we could have a trial. To see if your herd is as good as your pitch.'

'I ain't making no pitch, mister. I'm just giving you the plain truth,' said Bart. 'Why, the pony I work can outrun a storm.'

'Run faster than the wind? Now that's a critter I'd like to see.'

'Just step outside, sir. She's tethered to the rail.'

Calthrop immediately got to his feet and walked to the door. His hangers-on followed as did the four *bocarros*.

'That's Rolla,' said Bart, gesturing to a small-made palomino pony. 'She isn't big, she don't look much, but she's fleet and endurance should be her middle name.'

'And that's the critter that can keep ahead of a storm and run the competition into the ground?'

'Sure is.'

'Don't look so speedy to me. But there's only one way of finding out,' said Calthrop.

'And which way is that?' said Jess.

'A race. Whatever quality horse-flesh you got there, I'll lay good odds it don't compare with what we already got here. What d'you say?'

A ripple of interest ran through the small crowd that had gathered. Not much went on in Berry's

Crossing and the prospect of a little action raised the temperature.

'And what you got to put up against Rolla?' asked Jess.

'I'll show you. Nat,' said Calthrop, and he turned to one of his sidekicks, 'go get me the stallion.'

Nat stepped across the street to a wooden building with a sign Jebb's Stables and Livery over the door. A few moments later, he returned leading a tall black horse.

'This here is Prince,' said Calthrop, 'Three times champeen of Salt Creek County. Ain't no piece of horse-flesh this or any side of the Missouri got the legs of him. You talked big about your Rolla and now I'll do the same about Prince. I'm prepared to back him up heavy for a single mile dash. I'll lay you ten to one against your nag. I'll go you five hundred dollars against fifty that Prince will grind the little palamino into the dust.'

Voices in the crowd protested the odds were too long and wanted them shortened. Otherwise it wasn't hardly worth their while chancing their luck.

Jess, who'd been taking a look at Prince, took Bart to one side.

'Go easy on this, Bart,' he said. 'That's a strong horse he's got there. Never done a day's work; you can see he was bred for speed.'

'Maybe. But look at them great big haunches. I'd say he was pretty fast over a furlong or two but too heavy for distance work. Rolla will leave him stand-

14

ing. Anyways, I reckon I'm too deep into this to back down now. Got to go through with it.'

'Where you going to get fifty dollars for the stake?'

'I'll put up three, four horses from the herd, out of my share. They'll be more than good for fifty dollars. Anyways, I ain't counting to pay out on this.'

'What you waiting for?' asked Calthrop. 'Sure it isn't your nag but your tongue that can outrun the wind?'

The crowd laughed.

'Them odds is fine by me,' said Bart. 'You got yourself a race.'

The preliminaries were arranged. The course was measured out and agreed on. It ran from the Prairie Dog about a half-mile along the dirt road out of town to a single tree and back, to finish where they'd started from. Judges were chosen and the off was fixed for five o'clock, which would allow enough time for the news to get around and the townsfolk to come and watch and lay their bets, if they were so minded. But there were precious few takers for the odds of ten to one against Rolla. Calthrop produced his $500 dollars and Eli Hook went back to the drove and picked out three head that were adjudged well worth Bart's $50. The money and the ponies were deposited with old man Jebb the stableman, who acted as stakeholder.

Just before five o'clock by the starter's watch, Calthrop on Prince and Bart on Rolla lined up to the cheers of the crowd that had gathered to see the sport. Then the signal was given: 'One, two, three . . . go!' and they were off.

They had not gone fifty yards before Prince had opened a gap which grew wider with each stride. At 200, his lead had grown further and at 400 it was still growing. Prince reached the tree first and turned, with Rolla lagging so far behind that she seemed to have no chance. But the gap didn't grow any bigger and slowly began to get smaller. By the three-quarter mile mark, Prince was visibly tiring and Rolla was within striking distance. Another 200 yards and they were neck and neck. And then the little palomino passed the big stallion, although Calthrop had the whip to him, then left him further and further behind, eventually finished the course ahead by almost twenty yards.

The crowd cheered Rolla across the line an easy winner. Jess rightly judged the size of the cheer as an indication of how the townsfolk felt towards Reuben Calthrop. He took the filly by the bridle and Bart dismounted. Horse and rider, surrounded by the crowd, stood and watched Prince, in a lather, come panting in. Calthrop jumped out of the saddle breathing hard. He said nothing but his face, as black as thunder, made his feelings plain.

Old Jebb, the livery man, declared Bart the winner and said he could collect his winnings straight away, though if he so minded he could leave the ponies he put up for his stake with him, for a price to be agreed, if they were all in the same class as Rolla.

'And if the price is right,' he went on, 'I might jest mosey down to your corral and look over what you got. You did say you was in the selling business? My stock is getting low. It could do with some replenishment.'

'Be glad to see you,' said Jess. 'We'll be staying put a spell. You'd be welcome any time. And what say you, Mr Calthrop?' he went on. 'You reckoned the race was a kind of trial. Well, now you've seen what sort of animal we got for sale. . . .'

Calthrop's reply was to turn on his heel and, pulling hard on Prince's rein, dragged him clear of the crowd, hitched him to a fence post and started whipping him with his crop.

Prince rolled his eyes in fear and backed away from the man's flailing thong. But held by the rein, there was no escape.

Calthrop applied himself to his task with cold fury which grew icier still as the blood began to run down Prince's sides and back. Legs, belly, withers, the man lashed out as whatever target presented itself. The crowd was silenced by the cruelty of the sight of it. And all because Calthrop had been bested in an honourably conducted race by an opponent everyone agreed was a fair winner. It was only when Calthrop started on the horse's sensitive lips and nostrils and eyes that Bart stepped up to him and caught him by the arm.

'Hold it there. You want to blind your animal?'

Calthrop shook him off and whirled round with

murder in his face.

He dropped his whip, reached for his gun and fired at Bart twice before anyone was aware of what was happening.

Bart collapsed in a heap. Two growing patches showed glistening red on the front of his shirt, just over his heart.

'He attacked me,' said Calthrop, as cool as cool. 'You all saw it, you're all witnesses. Grabbed me from behind. A man's got a right to defend himself.'

He glared fiercely at the crowd which had been stunned by what had happened.

Jess dropped to his knees, stretched out one hand and felt for the beat of Bart's blood in his veins.

'He's dead! You killed him!' he said.

'Self-defence,' said Calthrop coolly. 'It was him or me.'

'He warn't attacking nobody,' said Eli Hook. 'He only tried to stop you killing your horse that never done you any harm except to lose you a race. . . .'

But his voice faltered as Calthrop turned and withered him with a glare.

'Anyone of you want to take it up for your friend? I'm willing to accommodate any one of you here and now.'

But he was backed up by his half dozen cronies and in a mood where he might do anything. There were no takers.

There was no law neither, so the matter ended there.

And that is how Bart Chandler died.

His body was given a burial by the *bocarros* who changed their plans, moved the herd on from Berry's Crossing the next day in hopes of finding a more welcoming town to rest up at.

The death of one man in a lawless territory where life is cheap is nothing way out of the ordinary. So why am I telling you all this?

My name is Chandler, Bradley Chandler.

Bart Chandler was my brother.

2

AMBUSHED

We heard the news from Jess, when he got back. But that was some time after Bart was shot dead at Berry's Crossing.

The *bocarros*, now reduced to just seven men, had moved on deeper into Kansas and sold the herd. Then they split up and went their separate ways. Some headed back West to try their hand at the same horse business again and the rest went on East hoping to get taken on by the government which always needed extra hands. Developing a territory isn't easy or simple, especially when there's not enough able men to do it.

Eli Hook, Billy Rively, Alban Slade and Zeke Hays heard tell of a government herd that had stampeded from Fort Benson and were running at large over the Kansas prairies and would revert to wild if not rounded up. A reward of ten dollars was offered for each head returned to the quartermaster. Inside a month, they had brought in nearly a hundred between them. It was good money and quicker and easier earned than rounding up, breaking and herding a drove from Colorado.

Then they heard tell that back East Majors & Russell, the biggest company of government freighters, were recruiting teamsters for wagon trains and paying them forty dollars gold a month. The deal was to guide and protect trains of twenty-five or more wagons laden with government supplies to provision the military outposts which grew up as the frontier moved ever westwards. It was a good deal for them. No one could blame them for going where the money was.

Jess reckoned he was getting too old to keep up with the youngsters and made for home. Jake Calberson and Sam Carter, being married men, also decided to call it a day and came back with him.

In addition to the news, Jess brought Bart's share of the money raised by the sale of the horses. It came to over $1000. He had tried to make Calthrop pay the $500 from the race he had lost, but Calthrop had refused, saying he would not honour a debt to a man who had tried to kill him.

All the family – Pa, Ma, Mary Sue and me – were all cut up, as you can imagine. Bart was a fine boy, good natured and straight as a die. I felt especially bad because, by rights, being older than him by two years, it was me who should have gone in his place.

21

But it was decided that since I was a better hand at tending to the farm and he at breaking horses, it made most sense for him to go.

We didn't have his body to bury, so we held a memorial service for him and put a cross up in the cemetery so he wouldn't be forgotten.

The $1000 dollars Jess brought was welcome. It was why Bart had gone droving in the first place. We needed the money.

At that time, Colorado was not a state. It wasn't even a settled territory and a man couldn't count on anything except himself. There was a lot of Indian trouble. But even if, like us Chandlers, you made peace with the tribes, you still had to look out for yourself. A man might put a fence around the claim he staked out, but that didn't mean a thing in law because there was no law to recognize a man's entitlement, not even to land he had cleared and worked. It was no different than if he was camping on it. Anyone with a gun could come along and send him and his family on their way if they were lucky, and to hell if they weren't, and simply steal what he had built up. There were some who were more than ready to shoot their way onto a ranch, keep it if they fancied or take whatever would fetch a price in Kansas, but either way would line their pockets at the expense of pioneers who had done all the hard work. Anyone with a mind to putting land under the plough or building up a herd of cattle or sheep with a view to making a future for his family for when

Colorado would become a civilized state, with laws and protection, had to be his own law and do his own protecting.

The railroad had not reached us yet, so land-hauled tools and other equipment were at a premium, such as the firearms we would need once the government got round to opening up the territory for settling. Because when that happened, there would be even more danger. We would have to defend our property with bullets or lose it. Settling a new territory is always a troublesome time. In Kansas, they'd almost had a civil war.

Maybe you're thinking us Chandlers took Bart's death a mite too easy, that me and Pa should have cleaned our guns, saddled our horses and gone after this Reuben Calthrop. I daresay some would have done it. But we were a God-fearing family. Besides, the farm couldn't be left to the womenfolk. Every hand was needed. So it was just as if Bart had died a soldier on some far-off killing field. Except he had not been fighting in a war between governments but for his own folk. Way we saw it, he had fallen in the struggle for survival that dominated our lives and would get a lot worse before it got better.

So as you can see, I was just a farm boy. Only thing I had ever killed was a rattler that frightened my horse or a prairie dog that got in among the cattle. Mind, I was never no Johnny Appleseed. I could look after myself. But I never went looking for trouble.

All that was to change.

In the spring after the fall when Jess got back, word went round that strangers had been seen spying out the land. They'd been asking enough questions for there to be no doubt: they were scouting out the valleys and plains that rumour said would soon be up for grabs in a free-for-all, winner-takes-all scramble for land when the politicians back East got round to fixing the settlement date. The people we knew, all our neighbours round about, started getting nervous. They thought about what precautions they could take. So did we.

Our place, the Chandler Ranch, was big. We were cattle mainly but we had fields under the plough too. Jess agreed to stay on and Jake Calberson and Sam Carter brought their families and we took on any useful man who asked for a job. This gave us enough hands to run things and also to put up a fight if that should prove necessary.

Our problem was still money for supplies. We needed it for wire to strengthen the fences bordering the ranch, for paying hired hands to do the job, and for more guns and ammunition.

Pa called a general council where it was agreed that one of us should join a drover team going east, then maybe sign up with Russell & Majors like the other boys had done, or go trapping for beaver pelts that would fetch seven dollars a piece. Take less than a year to clear good money that way.

Jess said no, he was too old and stiff. Jake and Sam said they'd left their families once and weren't

24

minded to do it again for so long a time. Besides, they weren't family and in their opinion if money was to be raised for the Chandler Ranch then it should be done by a Chandler. Since Pa was the only one who knew enough to run the place, that left me, the farm boy.

I said I would do it. But I wouldn't go droving for hire. I said there'd be more money to be earned if we rounded up our own ponies and employed our own team of drovers. Their wages wouldn't make much of a dent in the price we got for the stock. Pa agreed. So, for the next month and a half, four of us – me, Jake, Sam and a couple of hands passing through on their way west – chased down, roped and broke wild horses. In that time, we had rounded up near enough to 150 head and reckoned that would do us.

Then we needed drovers. I reckoned we could manage with four men in addition to myself.

Jake Calberson recommended a cousin of his, John. Eli Hook was back having had a losing streak in a poker game which had cost him near enough everything he'd earned fighting off Indians for forty dollars a month. He said he was in. That left two still to find.

One day I drove into Cedar Bluff to pick up some stores. I was loading up when I heard a ruckus coming from the Silver Dollar saloon. There was always trouble there. Cedar Bluff was still a frontier town and a stream of pretty tough customers passed through, some on the way to the prospecting hills where it was said fortunes could still be made, and others on the way back, having found nothing and saying there was no more gold there than in a newly robbed bank. And the Lucky Strike was the sort of place where a man who had got little return for his efforts was only too ready to vent his feelings on anyone who crossed him, especially when the whiskey had been flowing.

I joined some of the townsfolk who drifted towards the saloon in hopes of catching some of the fun. We didn't have to wait long. There was a crash of breaking glass and then a panhandler in red pants, big as a mountain, comes staggering out the door backwards and falls over, a look of surprise on his bloodied face. He picks himself up, dusts himself down, and back in he goes. The next moment, Billy Rively flies head first through a window and lands at my feet.

He was all for returning to the fray, saying how Cedar Bluff was his home town and how he wasn't going to let any fly-by-night stranger stop him having a drink when he wanted one. But he was no match for the big guy with the red pants, so I calmed him down and told him I was looking for drovers. His feeling for his home town soon cooled at the prospect of getting out of the place (everyone knew he couldn't stand his wife nor she him) and he said yes at once. He also introduced me to a friend of his, Pete Curtis, who was at that time looking for a berth. I had me a team.

We set out on the trail at the end of May. Two outriders, one on the left and one on the right, steered the herd while another ranged free, tidying up and rounding in stragglers as we went. One of us took turn to drive the supply wagon, drawn by a pair of mules, which brought up the rear.

At first, we made slow progress, the terrain being hilly and the going rough. But when we left the mountains and hit the plains, we picked up speed and it was easy work.

Maybe too easy.

A man can get careless. He can even nod off in the heat and the dust, lulled by the steady lollop of his horse, and hypnotized by the flat unchanging country. When there's nothing to see, you start thinking of nothing.

I guess I was to blame as much as anybody else, but no one spotted the Indians creeping up on us in the long buffalo grass until they were within easy range of the herd. We were all taken by surprise when they started hollering and whooping and firing their guns. One moment the sun was shining down on a peaceful landscape. The next, the herd had stampeded and bullets, arrows and feathered lances were flying.

It was hard to make out how many of them there were. Later, when I had time to count heads, there were about forty of them against the five of us.

We were in the middle of a wide plain. There was no hill or slough or trees within riding distance that could give us cover. The Indians had chosen their spot well, for if we tried to make a run for it they knew they would surely have the legs of us.

I was on wagon duty when it happened and I shouted for the others to forget the herd and join me. While they made for the wagon at a gallop, I cut the traces of one mule, led it to the left-hand side of the wagon and shot it through the head. It fell like it had been poleaxed. I did the same with the other, dropping it on the right-hand side. Then I dragged a couple sacks of flour from inside the wagon and propped them up at the back and front ends, not forgetting to smuggle a box of ammunition down between the wheels. We now had a kind of fortification and into it I crept. Resting my old Mississippi Yager on the belly of one of the mules, I succeeded in picking off a couple of the Indians who looked as if they would ride my comrades down.

They were the first men I had killed. I can't say I felt much about it one way or the other. There was too much going on.

As they reached the wagon, the boys dismounted in a hurry, slapped their horses on the rump with the flat of their hands to chase them off so the Indians wouldn't get them, and then joined me in our makeshift fort.

Our attackers still hoped to finish us off quickly. Luckily they only had a few guns and mostly they had bows and arrows and lances. Their shots were wild and most went wide into the long grass. But the body of the nearside mule was soon as spiky with arrows as a pincushion with pins.

'Let 'em have it, boys!' I shouted, when the leading riders were no more than thirty yards away.

They didn't need to be told twice.

The Indians' charge was suddenly halted in its tracks as three or four of them bit the dust and stayed there without moving.

We kept up our fire and got a few more of them. At this, our attackers, evidently puzzled at how to tackle a prey that had gone so effectively to ground, withdrew and gathered in a council, evidently deciding what to do next.

What they did next was to circle the wagon, just beyond the rage of our Colts. From time to time, one of them would kick his horse with his heels and make as if to come up to us. But at the first shots, he would turn and gallop back to the rim of the circle. One came to grief when his horse took a direct hit in the chest. It fell, throwing him on to the ground, then rolled over. The brave's gun was knocked from his hand and he ended up under his dead mount, trapped and out of action. But nothing else happened: it was a stand-off. After a while, at a given signal, they took up their previous station in front of the cart. The sun, now low in the clear sky, was at their backs. But it shone directly in our eyes.

'I don't like the look of this, boss,' said Eli Hook. 'They'll wait a spell till the sun's so low we'll be blind. Then they'll make their move. They'll inch forward without seeming to and be on us before we know what's happening.'

'Got any more ideas, Brad?' said Billy Rively. 'Smart move turning the wagon into a dug-out. I never saw it done before. Where d'you get the idea?'

'Never mind about that now,' I said. 'Anyone see what happened to our mounts?'

Billy said he could make out three horses with saddles in back of us grazing quietly in the grass which had now begun to sway in the evening breeze which strengthened as it blew over our heads and into the sun. They must have stopped running pretty soon and when it all went quiet they had drifted back. They were too used to being with men to go far. Pete made out a fourth and also a dozen or so bron-cos from the herd that had tagged along with them for company.

More than enough for a getaway.

Maybe it was the new respect I heard in their voices which told me they now thought of me as more than a farm-boy, but I felt a surge of excite-ment. And suddenly I knew what my next move would be.

'Right, boys. Here's what we do.'

The Indians were strung out in a line in front of us like the audience at a play, waiting for the sun to get low enough. Already they seemed a mite nearer every time you looked at them. With their minds on a stealthy frontal attack, they had not bothered to cover our flanks and rear. I told John Calberson to back out and open the keg of axle grease we carried and the others to grub up enough buffalo grass to make four or five torches. When they had enough, John smeared them with grease.

'What next, boss?' said Billy.

'What are they doing now?' I called to Eli, who was posted to keep track of their progress.

'Still shuffling forward. But I guess it won't be long now afore they charge. Wind's getting up and making the grass blow about, so it isn't easy to tell whether they're stopped or advancing.'

'Put a match to the torches. Then when they're well alight, throw them as far as you can in a fan shape. We're gonna put a prairie fire between them and us!'

Each man took a flaming brand and hurled it at the Indians. The torches formed a wide arc in the sun-dried grass which quickly started to blaze up in the wind which carried billows of smoke towards the Indians who let off a volley of shots to vent their fury. But their horses snorted with fear and soon their riders turned and fled before the advancing wall of fire.

I turned and saw grins on the faces of John, Pete and Eli who let go yippees to relieve their feelings. But of Billy there was no sign until Pete found him lying in the grass with a bullet through his shoulder. A stray shot had got him during that last wild salvo.

While the boys rounded up the horses before they too got scared by the flames and smoke and took off, I stopped the bleeding, bound the wound tight and strapped his arm up. The bullet would have to come out. It lay awkwardly and was best left till we found a doctor. Meanwhile, Billy was as comfortable as I could make him. He reckoned he'd be fine on a horse so long as we didn't move along too fast.

Leaving Eli and the boys to finish patching him up, I decided to take a look at the brave who had his horse shot from under him. He lay where he had fallen, on our side of the wall of fire, and I made out his gun a few yards off in the grass. He was alive and his black eyes glared defiance as I approached slowly. One arm was invisible under the horse and the other was nowhere near any knife that I could see. I picked up the gun and unloaded it. I fetched my horse and hitched it to his dead pony and pulled it off him. While I kept him covered, he sat up and felt himself all over. He seemed to have come to no harm. I took his knife from his belt and stuck it in mine. To be sure he couldn't do us any mischief, I tied him fast to one of the wagon's wheel until we were ready to go.

'What are you going to do with the Indian?' asked John Calberson. 'You can't leave him here to die and I won't have no truck with shooting a defenceless man. They're only following their natures, same as us.'

I felt exactly the same way. So when Billy had been sat on his horse and we were all ready to go, I cut the Indian free, gave him back his empty gun and threw his knife as far as I could into the long grass. Keeping him covered, I gestured that he was free to go.

He looked at me in surprise, then grinned and placed one hand on his chest. Then he was gone, fused with the deepening shadow. I figured we'd be long gone before he found his knife. Even Indians can't see in the dark.

Then, leaving all the supplies we couldn't carry to the coyotes and prairie dogs, we took off into the gathering night sure in the knowledge that if the Indians wanted to get on our trail, they'd have to ride for many hours to get round the fire and backtrack.

3

BERRY'S CROSSING

We headed off east, with the wind in our faces, across the plain, by the light of the rising moon.

There was no need to hurry now since the Indians were as effectively trapped behind the flames as if a giant wall had just fallen out of the sky and kept us apart. They'd have their work cut out to stay ahead of the galloping flames and wouldn't have much energy to waste thinking about us. We'd even had time to round up the broncos on our side of the burning barrier that had not run too far after the stampede. We gathered a couple of dozen or so. At twenty-five dollars a head or so, they'd give us a $400 stake, a hundred apiece. If we got to a town which was crying out for horseflesh, we'd get more, not a fortune, but enough to rent us a room and enough to eat until we figured out what to do next.

We drove our small herd for four, maybe five

34

hours, until the moon slid behind a bank of clouds. Then we stopped but did not make camp. The idea was we would just rest up a spell until it got light and then move on. You never know with Indians, and we'd left tracks they could follow with their eyes shut.

Eli Hook had travelled this route maybe half a dozen times. By his reckoning, the next stop on the trail was Wattrass, maybe three, four days' steady progress.

'Too far,' I said. 'Billy's going to need tending before then and get fixed up properly, or else we'll have a case of fever on our hands and then blood poisoning. That wound's not going to get better by itself. Any place nearer?'

Eli hesitated. Then he said, 'Sure. Could be there tomorrow, Brad, if that's where you really want to go.'

'Why wouldn't I want to go there?'

' 'Cos it's in Hemburg County. Just a little place. Berry's Crossing.'

'Where Bart got killed?'

'The very same.'

'Don't see we got much choice.'

'Brad. . . .'

'I know what you're thinking, Eli, how I'll look this Calthrop up, not like what I see, even the score some and then get us all into a heap of trouble. But you got no cause to worry. Most likely the guy's moved on. Stands to reason: man like that won't want to hang about a one-horse town when he could be having himself a lot more fun someplace else. I don't want no trouble getting in the way of what I come all this way to do. The folks back home are depending on me and I'll see it through. Anyway, like I said, we got to get Billy to a doc or he's a goner. So I guess it's all settled.'

And that's how I came to be, late one June afternoon, riding up the only street of Berry's Crossing, Hemburg County.

We'd corralled the horses in the same place where Bart had left them two years before. First thing I did was to send Pete to find the local sawbones. He came back with a man of science name of Pelling who wore a frock-coat and carried a smell of whiskey around with him. He had told Pete to buy a couple of bottles of strong waters at the store in town, to deaden the pain he would be forced to inflict on poor Billy if the wound was as bad as Pete made out. He poured just enough down Billy's throat to make him pass out and, while he waited for this to happen, drank the rest himself.

'Waste not, want not,' he muttered.

To be fair, it did not seem to affect him any.

When Billy was out cold, he poked around in his shoulder and finally dug out the slug. Then he bandaged the wound and stood up.

'That'll be five dollars. Best not move him for a couple of days. If he takes bad, you know where I live. Thanks for the drink, boys. So long.'

And off he went.

While this doctoring was going on, Eli had paid a

call on old Jebb at the livery stables to say we had something to sell that he might want to buy. Just as the doc was leaving, the old man rolled up ready to look our horses over. He took his time but in the end said he would take them all and offered us a fair price.

'Be obliged if you'd deliver. I got the space for 'em back of the stables. But at the minute I'm short of hands.'

Leaving John Calberson and Pete to keep an eye on Billy, me and Eli Hook drove the horses through town and into Jebb's back lot. Then he took us into his office to get paid. We were feeling good. We'd been ambushed by Indians and had come out of it not only in one piece but with a profit too. Not as big as we'd been reckoning on, but at least we were still there to count it.

Jebb had our money, as agreed, and handed it over. We shook his hand and left.

As we stepped into the sunshine, two men came up to us, big fellows. Both carried guns. One was wearing a deputy's star.

'Hold it there, strangers,' said the man with the badge. 'As I hear it, you had business with old man Jebb.'

'Could be you heard right, could be you heard wrong,' I said.

'Don't get smart with me, mister,' he said. 'This badge may be made of tin but it means the law, and you got to do what the law, which is me, Skate Skerritt, says.'

'And what has the law, which is you, Skate, got to say to a peaceable man who attends to his own business and doesn't mind anybody else's?'

'Cut the fancy talk. Where you get them horses you just sold?'

'I don't see why I should tell you anything, but I will. I got nothing to hide. Me, Eli here and two other *bocarros* drove them all the way from Pardy County, Colorado. Got jumped by Indians day before yesterday. Managed to save thirty head or so. Satisfied?'

'I heard tell how that number of broncos was rustled from the Bar-T ranch yesterday. Now what you got to say about that?'

'What I say, Skate, is that you hear tell of a lot of things that don't concern me. I never heard of no Bar-T and the only thing I ever rustled was a paper bag. So why don't you go flash your tin badge at someone smaller than yourself.'

Skate turned red in the face. A large vein stood out on his temple and throbbed.

Maybe riling a man with a badge and a gun wasn't a smart move. But I never liked a bully and I had done nothing that could be of any interest to the law.

'He don't mean no disrespect,' said Eli, before the pressure got so high it blew the top off Skate's head. 'My pardner's got a mouth that runs faster than his brains.' Then, yanking my arm, he started walking us away.

'Sure nice talking to you boys,' he said.

'Stop right there,' said Skate.

As he spoke the words, a gun appeared in his hand and it was pointing our way.

We stopped in our tracks. It wasn't that he'd got the drop on us, because we weren't carrying guns. Packing a gun isn't considered very friendly when you go calling on a man you're going to do business with.

'These boys are acting mighty suspicious,' said his companion, who had not spoken until now. 'You can't let them just walk away. The boss wouldn't like it.'

Skate wore the star but the other guy had the brains.

'What you think we should do, Nat?' he grunted, wrinkling his forehead with the effort of thinking.

'Maybe haul them in for questioning,' said Nat. 'But don't ask me: what do I know? You're the law.'

Still holding his gun on us, Skate said without hesitating, 'I'm taking you in. Sheriff wants to talk to you. Move it and no tricks. Keep to the middle of the street.'

Shepherded by Skate and Nat and their guns, we were marched down the middle of Berry's Crossing's only street. There weren't many folks about and those we saw sort of crept about their business as if anxious to get it over and done with as fast as possible so they could get off the street and go home again. It wasn't a good feeling. I hadn't noticed it when I rode in with Eli and the horses. Probably had my mind too much on what I was doing to pay attention. But now I could feel the fear in the air.

I wondered where it came from.

About halfway along the street was a one-storey wooden shack with SHERIFF painted in white above the door.

Nat opened the door, and Skate herded us inside with his gun.

As my eyes adjusted to the sudden gloom, I saw a pair of black boots, a desk on which the boots were resting, black trouser legs tucked into the boots, a gleam of red which turned into a scarlet sateen waistcoat, with a star that was silver, not tin, pinned to it, and above the star the mustachio'd face of a man of no more than thirty who was sitting at the desk on a chair tilted back as far as it would go. He was not wearing a hat. His hair was blond.

'What's all this, Skate? What you got there?'

I glanced across as Eli. His face was white, as if he'd seen a ghost, or maybe someone from his past he'd rather not be seeing again. It set me remembering. . . .

'Couple of strangers for you, Rube,' said Skate.

I'd remembered right: Reuben Calthrop hadn't moved on from Berry's Crossing. He'd stayed and taken it over. Now I knew why the population lived in fear. The only law in town was what Calthorp said it was and there was nothing anybody could do about it.

'They was in a huddle with old man Jebb,' Skate went on. 'Sold him a couple of dozen broncos. I seen them counting the money.'

'Men of business, eh?' said Calthrop. 'How much you make?'

'That,' I replied, 'is for me to know and you to find out.'

'I'll find out all right. Skate, see what he's got in his pockets – and don't think of trying to stop my deputy doing his duty, mister,' he said to me. 'Many a man's got himself shot while resisting the law.'

Since he was the man who had all the cards, I let Skate turn my pockets out. He counted the money.

'A mite over four hundred dollars,' he said, and put the wad on Calthrop's desk.

'Confiscated,' said the sheriff. 'It's evidence.'

'Evidence of what?' I asked.

'I'll think of something. But now it's the cells for you boys.'

'They said there was more of them,' said Nat.

'How many?' said Calthrop.

'Three,' I said. 'One's got a slug in his shoulder.'

'Where they at?'.

'Camped down by the creek.'

'Let them be, Skate. We got the ringleaders and we got the money. Why would we want more? Only make more paperwork. Sounds like a good day's work as it is. I'd say it was time we went off duty. We'll think what's best to do with them in the morning.'

'If you're holding us,' said Eli, 'you got to tell us on what charge. It's the law.'

'No it ain't,' said Nat. 'But since you want to know,

41

it's rustling. It's almost always rustling.'

'That's right,' said Rube. 'And we always give the accused man a fair trial before hanging him. Rustlers are no-good vermin. Lock 'em up, Skate. Then we'll go get us a bite to eat at the Prairie Dog.'

Eli and me were unceremoniously bundled into Berry's Crossing's only cell. Skate took the key from its nail on the wall, locked up, then put the key back. Then he, Calthrop and Nat went out the door leaving us to ourselves.

'He means it, Brad,' said Eli. 'I don't give a gopher's tail for our chances. Calthrop's a real wild one. In the morning, if he can wait that long, we'll be strung up with a noose round our necks and left dancing on air. I knew we shouldn't have come.'

'It's too late to say that. But you're right about one thing: we got a problem. We can't stay here. Think we can bust out?'

We both started examining our cell. Though the front office was wood-built, the cell at the back was made of three mortar and stone walls. One had a barred window in it. The fourth, facing the office, was an iron grill with an opening section which was the door in and out. The floor was stone flagged.

'Looks pretty strong to me,' I said. 'Even if we had a pick, that wall would take some getting through.'

'What about the keys?' said Eli. 'Any way we can get them off that hook?'

'Too far. Must be thirty feet. But maybe the lock

ain't as strong as it looks. You got anything to pick it with?'

Eli bent down, fiddled with his boot and produced a piece of fencing wire.

'Thank the Lord for a busted boot,' he grinned, 'and my good sense in mending it with this darling little wire-end.'

While he worked on the lock, I took a peek through the barred window. Outside was a bare patch maybe twenty yards long squared off by low wooden palings. Beyond them I could see emigrants who had pitched their tents and parked their wagons. I heaved on the bars which rattled some but were pretty solid set into the wall.

The best of the day was done, but it would not be dark for a spell.

I turned to check on how Eli was doing.

'It's tricky. Question of getting the wire in the right position and using the right amount of force. Damn thing slips each time I try to turn it.'

After I while, I replaced him with the wire.

Then he tried again. But the wire had been weakened with all the poking and twisting and snapped off.

All this had taken some time and by now the light was fading fast. Soon it would be dark. We resigned ourselves to wait.

Suddenly, there was a low rustle and a voice whispered, 'That you, Brad?'

'Sure is, and mighty glad to hear a friendly voice!'

It was Pete Curtis and he had John with him.

'Eli in there with you? Good. Take this rope and fix it round the bars. We got four horses here and we're going to make a hole in the wall so you two jailbirds can fly away.'

While I wound the rope around the bars and secured it, Pete said that when old man Jebb had seen us being walked off by Skate and Nat, he knew we were in deep trouble. He'd gone out to the camp and told him and John they'd better get us out of jail if they wanted to see us alive again. The boys had come up with this plan. They broke camp, leaving it to look as if they'd left in a hurry and weren't coming back. The old man said he'd hold their horses for them. He'd told them about a tumbledown barn where Billy could hide up. He'd be safe there until Eli and me had been sprung. Then we could all go get him and the horses and hightail it out of Berry's Creek. They'd waited till it was dark enough and then made their move.

'Stand clear,' said Pete, 'the horses are taking the strain.'

I heard John urging the horses.

The bars began to bend outwards, but didn't give.

John and Pete rested the horses, then set them on again.

This time the bars began tilting up from the bottom, slowly, gradually, and then there was a creaking and a rending and suddenly they and a sizeable chunk of wall weren't there any more. Instead, there was a cloud of dust which filled my eyes and throat. As the air cleared, I blinked my eyes clear and began to make out stars in the night sky. I heard Eli's voice. But he wasn't cheering or whooping. What he said was, 'Brad, watch your back!'

I turned and saw three guns trained on us.

The hands holding them belonged to Skate, Nat and Calthrop, who smiled and said, 'Couple of minutes later and we'd have missed the party. But now the gang's all here, we can really make things go with a bang.'

Skate and Nat were just drunk. But Calthrop was nasty drunk.

4

BREAK-OUT

Calthrop told Skate to open the cell door. There didn't seem much sense in keeping anybody locked up in a cell that had no more backside to it than an apple-scrumping kid's pants.

Then he ordered Nat to go out back and find out who'd been wrecking his jail. Nat sobered up some, but he was still pretty slow in his movements.

Skate had some difficulty fitting the key in the keyhole. He held it in one hand and waved it around so much that I was afraid the gun he had in the other would go off and kill somebody, and that somebody could have been standing on either side of the bars. When he finally inserted it into the lock, it got jammed by the end of the wire Eli had broken off inside it, and when he couldn't get it out again he swore, lost his temper and shot the lock off anyway. Then he stumbled into the cell and lunged at Eli, grabbing him and pushing him out. He gave me the same treatment then sat down, blowing hard. He looked around vacantly. Next moment his eyes had closed and he had passed out.

One down, two to go.

But though the odds had improved they were still too long.

The time Skate took hustling us out of the cell was long enough for Nat to take a look-see and come back.

'All quiet out there now, Rube,' he reported. 'Only folks about was emigrants and they weren't saying if they saw anything. Must be blind and deaf if they didn't catch on to what was going on. We'll ask again tomorrow. Get some answers then. But they certainly made a mess of the wall. Pulled most of her down.'

'No need to go bothering the neighbours,' said Calthrop turning to us, 'when we got witnesses here who can tell us what happened. You,' he barked at Eli, 'what happened? Who did it? How many were there of them?'

'Couldn't rightly say,' said Eli. 'I'm not a tall guy and the window was too high for me to see out of. I didn't hear anything until the bars were pulled off her. . . .'

Eli was right. He wasn't tall. But Calthrop was. Bigger too, and heavier. So when he chopped Eli with a right and followed up with a left, you could hear bone break. Eli went down and didn't get up.

'How about you, mister? You got fancy answers, or

are you going to tell me who did this thing?'

It turned out he didn't really want to hear any answers, fancy or otherwise. What he wanted was to get back at somebody for thinking they could put one over on him. Anybody would do, and I was there.

I was about to tell him some yarn that would take attention away from Pete and John and give them time to get further away when he suddenly lashed out without warning and connected with a left that caught me on the ear. I was taken by surprise. I staggered back and fell over a chair. Before I could get up, he was on me, wading in with his boots.

I felt a rib go and curled up to protect my face and chest.

Then he changed tack and straightened me up with a good toe-kicking in my back.

I tried scrambling away, thinking I could get on my feet. But Nat now joined in and started working on my legs.

There was nothing I could do about it. After a while, I felt myself slipping away.

I don't know how long they kept it up. I reckon not too long after I passed out. They'd been going at it pretty hard for some time and they were pretty drunk to start with. So I guess they must have lost interest in me after a while, though they gave Eli a going over too. He wasn't a big guy and they hurt him real bad.

When they'd punched and kicked themselves out, they most likely went back to the Prairie Dog for another drink. At least I guess that's where they went. But wherever it was, they weren't there when I came to. I was hurting all over. The noise made when I breathed told me my nose was staved in and when I tried to sit up I knew a few more ribs had gone too. My arms and legs had taken such a pounding that the muscles were swollen and it was agony trying to move them. My left arm felt like it was broken but both legs still seemed in one piece. But that I wouldn't know for sure until I got up and stood on them, something I thought I might manage within the next year or two, but not in the near future. That gives you an idea of the sort of job they'd done on me. But I thought I should try. I started by rolling over on one side and got hit by shooting pains in my back where they'd battered my kidneys. I was a mess.

But not so much a mess as Eli. He was lying like a rag doll on the floor. One leg was twisted unnaturally under him and his face was an unrecognizable bloody mess. I studied him from where I was. After a while, I knew for sure he wasn't breathing.

Slowly, I moved my arms, my legs, my neck. Strong men in fairs win ten dollars for making less effort than I did for heaving myself up on one elbow. Then after another spell to catch my breath, I sat up.

It was only then that I realized what a fix I was in.

I had no idea how long Calthrop and his cronies had been gone. But even with my brains scrambled the way they were I knew they'd be back to finish the job. With Eli dead, they couldn't afford to leave a witness alive to shoot his mouth off and make trouble. But I was in too bad a way to work up enough enthusiasm to figure out what to do next. Most of my concentration went on breathing.

I finally got myself upright but soon realized I'd made a mistake: I preferred being on the floor. It was safer. So down I went again in a heap, waiting for the world to stop spinning. Putting weight on both legs had told me that neither was busted, that was something, but if I was going anywhere, I knew I'd have to do it on hands and knees. I also knew that if I was going to crawl any place, I couldn't afford to wait. If I wasn't out of there and away by the time they got back, then that was two Chandler boys Calthrop would have murdered.

This thought put some urgency into the situation.

I shuffled as best I could over to Eli.

When I was sure he was dead, I told him goodbye. He'd been a good friend to me and I made a friend's promise to take retribution on his killer.

But if I was going to make that promise good, I was going to have to be in better shape than I was now. I had to get away – to fight another day. The verse went round and round in my head. It helped straighten up my thoughts.

Maybe Calthrop hadn't locked the door. Why bother? He had left two men in it, one dead and the other as good as. But the door led into the street and the street was not a good place to hide. What about the back way?

Skate had shot the lock off the cell door which still hung open. Beyond it was the gaping hole Pete and John had made in the wall. I remembered that empty squared-off patch outside and the emigrants who had been unhelpful to Nat. The sun had set long ago, the moon was not yet up and it was now very dark.

I decided to go out the back way.

I dragged myself across the floor and into the cell. When I reached the wall, I hauled myself up by my right arm and let myself fall through the hole. That got most of me outside. When the pain subsided and let me think again, I pulled the rest of me through, negotiated a way across the rubble and began crawling across the square patch.

When I'd looked at it through the cell window, I'd guessed it was maybe twenty yards to the paling at the far end. I must have got it wrong. From ground level, with a busted arm and cracked ribs, it looked like a prairie and the palings were some distant horizon at least twenty miles away. But I got there.

I was even able to pull myself up by a paling post and climb over. Telling myself I was a man and that men walked on two legs not four, I leaned against the fence and looked around.

Nobody was about. The emigrants' tents and wagons were dark. Maybe they'd gone to bed early. More likely they were keeping their heads down.

I took a few groggy steps. I didn't like the feeling and stopped. But a breeze had started up. It cooled my face and blew some of the cobwebs out of my head.

Hold it right there, pardner, I said to myself. No sense just walking. Got to work out where would be a good place to walk to. That was a hard one.

Then I got the idea that riding was better than walking. That breakthrough didn't tell me where I should head for, but it made me see that wherever I was going I'd get there quicker on a horse than on my own two feet. I remembered I had a horse once. When was that? Must have been . . . Got it! I'd come to town on a horse. With Eli and the broncos. To clinch the deal with old man Jebb.

Jebb's Livery. That's where I'd left it. It would still be there.

I felt a lot steadier now I had a purpose.

There was a loose paling in the fence. I pulled it off and tucked the end under my right shoulder. That way I got along much faster. I could have been entered for a race with snails and stood a good chance of winning.

Keeping the backs of the building that fronted onto Berry's Crossing main street to my right, I shuffled along, easily covering a three minute walk in twenty. When I got to the back of Jebb's, I found that the gate Eli and me had taken the broncos through was shut up for the night. I rattled the lock in frustration. To come this far, and be denied was about as much as I could stand.

Then a voice said, 'Who's that? What you want?'

I recognized old Jebb's voice.

'Brad Chandler. I left my horse here. I need it. Let me in.'

I heard a rattle of keys, a lock being turned and the gate open. I fell through it. The old man caught me before I hit the ground and laid me down gently. He called out softly and moments later I felt myself being carried into the office where we'd done our deal all amicably just a few hours before.

Jebb and Jebb's man gave me a shot of whiskey and cleaned me up some.

'You look a mess, boy,' said the old man. 'They gave you a good roughing up. Where's your friend?'

'Eli? Dead. They kicked him to death. If I'd stayed they'd have done the same to me. That's why I need my horse. Got to get away – fight another day.'

'Where's Calthrop and his thugs now?'

'Ain't sure for certain. Maybe they went back to the Prairie Dog to fire themselves up some more.'

'Hank,' said Jebb, 'go take a peek in the saloon and see if Calthrop's there.'

While Hank was gone, he left me to rest. I had just starting to float off down a quiet stream on some feather-soft raft which was being wafted along on a warm breeze when something shook my arm.

'Wake up,' said Jebb. 'Calthrop's drinking in the saloon and he's fighting drunk and meaner'n hell. You're in no fit state to go anywhere but you sure as Hades can't stay here. You got to get out of town, and fast. When he's ready, he'll go back to his office.

When he sees you've gone, he'll start looking for you. On your feet. I've saddled your horse.'

He told me how to get to the barn where the boys had taken Billy and wished me good luck.

With a hand up from Hank, I got on to my horse and rode out of Jebb's yard.

I don't know if I made much noise, but it didn't matter, because I'd soon left Berry's Crossing and was out on the road where there was no one to hear me. Old Jebb's directions had gone clean out of my head. So I took a bearing by starlights which pricked little holes in the blackness above my head and slowed to a canter and then, when I started hurting again, to a walk.

The motion was restful and there was a rhythm to it that got inside my head, going round and round to a chant which turned into words: got to get away to fight another day. I'd nod off and then be jolted back to wakefulness when a rib reminded me of its presence by shooting a pain across my chest.

As I crested a rise, I stopped to take another mouthful from the bottle Jebb had given me. I wasn't minded to dismount, because I didn't think I'd be able to get back on again. The whiskey warmed me up and dulled the pain some. As I took a last mouthful, I looked down the length of the bottle and in the distance saw a cloud of dust, as if there were riders coming my way. They were travelling fast.

They were too far away for me to tell how many they were. But they were following the trail I'd taken and would soon be upon me. In the state I was in, there was no way I could outrun them. I couldn't even raise a gallop without passing out.

I turned and scoured the way ahead for cover, a place to hide up until they'd gone by.

About 500 yards further along, the trail dipped, crossed a stream and then went on through a pile of giant boulders, like a mountain pass only not on such a large scale. Maybe 2–300 yards off left was a copse of soapwood trees big enough to hide half a dozen horses. Not quite as far away on the right-hand side was a smaller patch of brushwood covering a raised mound. I seemed spoiled for choice.

But it wasn't necessarily so. The pass through boulders was fine for an ambush, but I was in no shape for a fight. I needed to lie low and let the danger blow over. Since the copse was the first real cover on the road for a mile or two, I figured that whoever was trailing me might think it worth their while to spare a few minutes to check it out. That left the mound. It wasn't perfect but it was my best shot.

I urged my horse along the trail and crossed at the stream. Then I struck lucky. After about ten yards the trail on the other side became bare rock that would not show any trace of my passage. It would be hard to read my tracks. An Indian could do it, but not a bunch of red-eyed white men with too much liquor in them. I reckoned they'd figure I'd ridden on ahead and take off after me. Then I'd have time to work out which way I should go to put as many miles between them and me as I could.

I left the stream and rode on for a couple of dozen yards. Then I stopped, retraced my steps and went this way and that on the bank, creating many tracks that led every which way. Next I rode back into the stream and turned along it, leaving it only when I reached a point opposite the mound. I headed straight for it. A real scout would have no difficulty working out where I had gone, but it was the best I could do in the circumstances.

The mound was high enough to hide my horse. I dismounted with difficulty and tethered him to a bush. He started to graze. I crawled on my belly and looked over the top.

I had a good view of the crossing which was maybe a hundred yards off. The moon was high and bright and it turned the land a bluey-silver colour.

I had not long to wait.

The first I heard of the horses was the sound of hoofs which came like the dull roar of a distant torrent. Then I saw their dust, a cloud which grew bigger the nearer they came. Then I picked out three galloping horses and finally their riders. The moon glinted on something one of the men wore on the front of his shirt. It had to be a badge.

The riders reached the stream and halted. They stared at the ground, unable to make anything of the tracks. One rode along the stream towards the soapwood copse, looking down at both banks as he went. When he got there, he dismounted and looked for tracks in the sandy earth. He stayed where he was a while but when he found nothing, he rode back to the others. A second men came along my stretch of the stream but gave up while he was still a good way off. The third rider cantered along the trail through the boulders. After a while he came back too. My trail had died on them. I could hear the sound of voices but couldn't make out what they were saying. But it was clear they were arguing. One of them (Calthrop, I supposed) wanted to go on. But the others wanted to call off the chase.

In the end, Calthrop won. And all three rode off.

I lost sight of them after they entered the pass between the boulders. But I went on hearing the sound of their horses which grew fainter and fainter and finally disappeared.

By that time, finally able to stand my defences down, my aching body had got the better of me. I did not relax so much as pass out.

When I came to, the sun was high. But that wasn't the first thing I saw.

What I saw was the face of an Indian looking down at me.

And the tomahawk in his hand which was aimed at my head.

5

DEATH IN A
QUIET CANYON

I watched helplessly as the tomahawk scythed down. Instinctively I shut my eyes, turned away and tensed my muscles against the inevitable.

Even that movement was torture. My legs complained, my ribs made me wince and my broken arm was such agony that I almost passed out again. I thought they were the last sensations I would ever feel.

Then I heard a thud on the ground near my right ear. The Indian had missed!

I opened my eyes and saw him raise his tomahawk again. But instead of striking a second blow, he was looking at the blade, now wet and glistening. He wiped the blood off it and returned it to his belt.

Then he knelt beside me and pointed at something on the ground where I had heard the thud.

I turned my head and found myself looking directly into the evil face of a rattlesnake. A dead one.

He said something in his language. I didn't understand, but I didn't need to. It was as plain as if he'd drawn me a picture. He'd seen the rattler crawling in my direction to investigate. He had crept up on it and, just as I regained consciousness, he had removed its head before it could strike.

Then he broke into a broad smile and started jabbering in his lingo.

Now I was in no state for long parleys with my best friend, let alone with an Indian I could not understand. I'd had dealings with Indians back home and had picked up a few words. I managed to pick out *isantanka*, meaning an American, *hoecah* (surprise) and sufficient others to gather that he was amazed but pleased to see me. Later I would have plenty of opportunity to learn the Indian language of his tribe. But just then, he might as well have been talking Chinese.

When he saw the blank looks I gave him, he stopped, reached for his belt and took out his knife. I tensed again but he reassured me with a gesture. He mimed throwing it away and suddenly I knew him.

He was the Indian who had been thrown by his horse when the hostiles had stampeded the herd and cornered us under the wagon.

And he was grateful, so grateful he tried to pull me upright. I nearly passed out again.

He stopped when he saw how badly hurt I was.

'*Aie! Kakeshya?* (How terrible! Have you been tortured?)'

That was one way of putting it, I suppose.

I made signs that I was thirsty. I also felt hot. A man don't take a beating like the one I'd been given without feeling the effects. My busted arm seemed to be burning up and I was suddenly afraid that if it wasn't tended to soon, I could lose it.

'Can't move this arm,' I said. 'It's broke.'

He didn't understand my words either, but he got my meaning plain enough. He said something that meant I should stay right where I was.

'I ain't going no place,' I said.

He disappeared into the brushwood where I heard him beating around. When he returned, he was trimming a branch of brushwood about a foot and a half long. He cut strips off the sleeve of my shirt and used them to bind the splint lengthwise on my arm, just like I'd seen my Pa do when one of us or a hired man bust an arm or a leg.

I'd rather not recall the time he spent doing it. It wasn't his fault it hurt so much. He was careful enough. But the break was maybe sixteen hours old and had become inflamed.

I guess I must have passed out again.

But he revived me with another drink from his waterskin and managed to prop me on my horse. He had no horse and led mine.

Later he told me he was not mounted because he was still making his way on foot back to his tribe after the attack on our wagon.

I can't say I remember much about that trip, nor of the way I was treated when we got back to the place where his tribe was camped. It must have been a good few days before I became aware of what was going on around me.

When I woke, I found myself staring up at a smoke-hole at the apex of an Indian tepee. I was lying naked on a couch raised a few inches from the floor under a buffalo skin which was as hot as Hades and smelled like the fleece room in a tannery. When I moved my legs, they didn't hurt at all now. But my arm throbbed and, when I tried to sit up, the pain in my ribs took my breath away.

An old crone squatted at the fire in the middle of the tepee stirring something in a pot with a wooden spoon. When she saw I was back in the land of the living and trying to get up off my couch, she turned in my direction.

'*Anoptah! Bes!* (Stop! Be careful!)' she said.

She made me lie back and then spooned some of what she had been stirring in her pot down my throat. It tasted like pond scum would taste if you went to the trouble of warming it up. I tried to brush her off, but she was strong and I was pretty weak, and all the time she kept spooning and saying words which I didn't understand but doubtless were no different from what Grandma used to say when she used to make us take our medicine when we were little.

And, like Grandma, she knew best and was right. My nose stayed out of shape and didn't make me look any prettier. But the fever had gone and didn't come back, my arm began to mend and my ribs turned merely sore and then stopped hurting altogether.

I grew stronger and started to take notice. One day, I received a visit.

Squawking Crow, the brave who had rescued me in return for saving his life, had continued to take an interest in me and came to see me pretty regular. I picked up a few words from him and the old woman, but not enough to say more than how the weather was good or bad or how I was getting on. But one day, he came with a tall, powerful-looking Indian in ceremonial regalia and full headdress. This was Kla Klitso, 'He-who-has-copper', Chief of the Kepwejo. He was called this on account of the necklace he wore made of spent copper bullets fired by fusees, those old flintlock muskets they used to use in the fur-trade.

I got up best I could, to show respect, and said, 'How!'

With a gesture, he said, 'White man sit.'

I sat on the buffalo skin. He sat on another, crosslegged and stared at me.

Turned out he could speak English more than moderately.

With an Indian, you take time over the preliminaries. I said how it was a great honour for me to be in his camp and so well received. I said that, seeing how I came to be there, I was sorry I had no gifts for him.

He waved his hand.

I told him how I regretted not being able to tell Squawking Crow thanks for saving my life twice, once from the rattler and once from the effects the beating I'd had.

He brushed my words aside and said that Squawking Crow could never repay his debt to me, 'Bringer-of-Fire', as I was now known in the camp. The life I had saved was mine for all time.

I said I was sorry we'd killed those young men of his tribe, but they had attacked us without provocation and shot one of my friends.

This, too, he waved away, saying the braves had been acting on their own, not on his orders. They had courage to spare, but acted before they thought. He said he hoped they'd learned something.

'The guns we have, no good,' said. 'Too old. One shot only each. That day the braves were young and foolish. Is of no account. Is finished now.'

Then he guffawed as he told me how far they had ridden before they managed to get away from the burning buffalo grass that chased them and how they'd come back to camp smelling of smoke and looking foolish.

He said his tribe had always lived on peaceable

terms with the *Isantanka*. That is until white men
from Berry's Crossing had started acting hostile,
driving them off their land, manhandling any braves
who went into town and even on occasion riding
through their camp, setting fire to their lodges and
shooting their animals.

'Why they do this thing? Land is for all. Also game.
Better trade than fight. But *millahanska* bad. So we
fight him. Braves of tribe attack you. Braves think you
go with horses to sell to see *millahanska*. For this they
attacked. All hate *millahanska*.'

The Indians I knew back home were peaceful too.
But I knew what they were capable of when they felt
threatened.

I saw Kla Klitso many times during the time it took
for me to get my strength back. Out of the talks we
had I built up a picture of a reign of terror kept up
by the men from Berry's Crossing, and especially the
one he called *millahanska*. At first I could make nothing of this. I guessed the words meant something like
'White-man-with-silver-shining'. Did he mean a man
with white hair? But when I got him to describe who
he meant, he came up with a suit of black and a vest
of red. Of course! Calthrop, the white man with a
silver star!

From other things he told me, it became clear that
Calthrop had taken over Berry's Crossing and was
using it as a cover for criminal operations of all kinds.
His ranch, the Bar-T, was his headquarters. He had
maybe twenty or thirty men working for him. Some

were cowhands and bronco breakers, for the Bar-T
had acquired a lot of stock which was regularly got
up into herds and driven east to be sold to the army,
who always needed beef and mounts, or to the population mushrooming along the Santa Fe trail. But
some of his men did no ranching work and wore
guns. Calthrop paid them well, so they had no
complaints. From the Bar-T, he'd take off from time
to time and ride mostly east where new settlements
were springing up and stage-coach runs, even rail-
roads were reaching. Then a week or so later, he'd be
back with a loaded wagon or a string of horses he
hadn't had before. Putting the pieces together, it
wasn't hard to work out that Calthrop and his boys
were on to a good thing, robbing banks, stopping the
stage, raiding trains and attacking trading posts. He
also made those emigrants who were unlucky
enough to stop in Berry's Crossing pay a 'passing-
through' toll, a tax levied for driving along local
trails, drinking the local water, setting up camp on
local ground and, for all I knew, for breathing the
local air.

There was no one in Berry's Crossing strong
enough to stand up to him. And since he'd
appointed himself sheriff, he was beyond the reach
of the law.

It was a pretty good set up.

At the start of the time when I was still building
myself up and getting fit again with the Kepwejo,
there was an incident which gives some idea of the

tensions surrounding the place and explains the source of the fear I had smelled the first time I'd come up against King Calthrop.

Now, the Kepwejo stayed well away from town when Calthrop was around. But they always knew when he'd gone foraging for booty and chose those times to transact their business at the Indian agency at Berry's Crossing. But on this occasion, Calthrop had returned sooner than expected and caught out a couple of braves who'd gone into town to trade a load of pelts for a sack of flour and a few pounds of salt. As they left the Agency, they were stopped by half a dozen of Calthrop's men who took them to the saloon, got them drunk and poured their flour and salt into the road for entertainment. Then they let them go. Didn't even rough them up. I took this as a sign they were in a good mood. The raid they'd been on must have paid off pretty good for them to be so jovial.

The young braves were all for riding into town there and then and settling the score. Kla Klitso talked them out of it. It wasn't that he was any less keen than they were. But the Kepwejo just didn't have the fire power and if it came to a showdown it was a sure bet that only the slow old men would be left alive: a tribe consisting of old timers, women and children had no future. But he knew he wouldn't always be able to keep them on a leash. One day they'd be pushed too far, they'd break out and there'd be nothing he could do to stop the carnage.

As the weeks went by I slowly felt my strength returning. After a spell, the old crone weaned me off the murky brews she cooked up in her cauldron and gave me buffalo steaks instead. This brought me on a lot faster. A man needs meat.

Meanwhile, I wondered where Pete and John had gone with Billy. Where was this safe place they'd talked about?

I told Kla Klitso I was worried about my friends. He sent a couple of braves to take a look-see. They said the white men had stayed a spell in a broken-down old barn on a farm belonging to 'He-who-has-horses' (I guessed they meant old man Jebb) which he only used for grazing his stock. But they weren't there any more.

I couldn't find out how Billy had got on. But I guessed that whether there were two or three of them they'd either gone back home or moved on. No way could they come looking for me. How could they? I was the only white man in the whole wide world who knew where I was.

One day, Squawking Crow took me out riding. I was getting stronger now, though my arm was still sore sometimes and I didn't have the full use of it yet. I reckoned I could hurry my recovery along if I stopped sitting around and pushed my body hard as I could.

We galloped the horses and took turns jumping boulders and tilting at steep slopes. My arm was holding up pretty well and I felt good about it. We were about to thread our way through a narrow passage between fallen boulders into a canyon Squawking Crow knew about where a rider could be put through some tough trials. Suddenly he stopped dead and pointed at the ground.

There were tracks of mules, maybe four or five of them, and two newly shod horses. They were recent, and they went one way. Unless there was a back way out, the party which had left the tracks must still be in the canyon.

He slid off his pony and led it into a patch of tall mesquite. He gestured for me to do the same.

When both horses were tethered, he snapped a branch he'd cut off a bush and used it to sweep our tracks clear behind us. We retreated like this until we were among loose scree at the foot of the bluff. This we climbed until we were maybe fifty feet above the narrow passage that led between the boulders into the gorge.

Keeping to about the same height, we followed a narrow ledge that led around the shoulder of the bluff until we reached a point where we had an uninterrupted view of the canyon. We moved forward slowly, choosing where we put our feet: a stone dislodged would turn into a minor avalanche and give our location away to anyone who might be watching. Squawking Crow went first. He kept his head down and stopped to listen from time to time for any warning sound.

There was no back way out. What we found was a

natural bowl surrounded on four sides by a high rim of bare rock that was almost sheer at the top but sloped down in easy steps until it reached the *arroyo*, the Mexicans' name for the bed of a dried-up water-course. When the place was hit by a sudden storm, the water would rush down the steep sides of this natural basin, collect at the bottom and force a way out through the boulders in the narrow pass below us which was the only way in and the only way out. A couple of armed men could have held it indefinitely. But no one was posted among the boulders and in the valley below us there was not a soul to be seen.

Squawking Crow stared hard, his brow furrowed. He couldn't make sense of it.

The tracks had shown that horses had come in and not gone out. Yet the canyon was deserted.

Then he touched me on the arm and pointed.

From the height we were at, there was no way even he could follow the tracks for more than a few yards from the entrance to the pass. They were lost among the loose stones of the dry water-course. But by following the course of the stream he had noticed other traces – a bush with a branch hanging oddly as if something had brushed against it, a rock in the bank that had been disturbed and left unnaturally balanced – which led towards a projection or rocky spur.

I nodded to indicate I'd spotted the signs too.

The spur blocked our view of where the trail might have led. To get a better look, Squawking Crow moved a few yards to his right, still in a crouch, making for the shelter of a medium-sized boulder. He never made it.

There was the crack of a rifle and he went down like a rag doll.

I didn't even think about going to help him.

Dead men don't need help.

6

BURIED ALIVE!

Squawking Crow fell in a heap. Then his body began to slide down the steep face of the hill, gathering speed as it went. The crack of the shot that killed him was still reverberating around the canyon when his body slowly came to a stop on the bank of the dried-up river bed about forty of fifty feet below me.

I didn't move. I hadn't seen where the shot had come from. Nothing moved for a long spell after which there was more nothing.

I didn't move, either. For all I knew, the same gun that killed Squawking Crow, or a different gun, it made no difference, might be pointing at me.

All this time I had my own gun out of its holster, but there was nothing to shoot at.

Then, an hour at least after the sun had passed overhead, I saw something move.

Above the rocky spur where Squawking Crow had

lost sight of the trail was a stretch of ground that sloped up gently among a litter of boulders. In the middle was a patch of mesquite growing round a boulder. What had caught my eye was the glinting barrel of a rifle that had suddenly poked out of the bushes.

I still had nothing to shoot at.

Then the branches shook and a head appeared. It was Nat, Calthrop's main man.

I held my fire. Where Nat was, Calthrop would not be far behind. I was right.

Looking round him all the time and keeping his rifle up, Nat came out of the bushes. He took a look at Squawking Crow and seemed satisfied there was no one else about. He gave a signal and Calthrop followed him out.

'All clear,' said Nat, putting up his gun.

I had the two of them in my sights. I took a bead on Calthrop and pulled the trigger. At this range I couldn't miss. My Colt gave a dull click as the hammer hit the firing-pin. The sound was too low to be heard above the sighing of the afternoon wind which had got up. The two men below me gave no sign of alarm and went on with their business which just then consisted of leading a string of mules out of the mesquite.

I cursed silently and flipped open the chamber. It was empty!

I had every reason to be grateful to the Indians who had saved my life, but just then I would have gladly throttled every last light-fingered man jack of them. For a joke they'd hide my hat or fill my boots with sand. They also 'borrowed' on a permanent basis anything that took their fancy. They didn't have the same notions of property.

No excuses. It was my fault. I should have checked. I had missed the best opportunity a man could have wished for to rid the world of a prime skunk.

Nat was below me now, walking the mules towards the pass that led out of the canyon. Calthrop brought up the rear with their horses.

I reached for the ammo in my belt. But I had stayed still for so long that my muscles were cramped and my movements were slow and clumsy.

As I was wasting time loading my gun, my best chance of a clear shot disappeared.

Nat glanced down at the body of Squawking Crow and said, 'What's the chances he wasn't alone? You reckon he had friends with him?'

'Nope,' said Calthrop. 'We didn't see any and no one came looking for him. He was by himself and a lone Indian don't signify.'

I dropped a couple of slugs in the chamber and snapped it shut.

But they were gone.

Or at least they were out of sight. But maybe one of them, just to be sure, was hidden behind a rock ready to take a pop at anything that moved. I was too exposed. It wasn't worth the risk. I'd catch up with Calthrop soon enough. He'd not stray far from his set up at Berry's Crossing. He'd invested too much time and energy in it. For the time being I was more interested in finding out how they'd managed to hide themselves and seven horses in a patch of mesquite.

I let more time trickle by.

When I figured it was safe, I stood up, stretched to get the circulation going again, then made my way back along the steep shoulder we had come in by until I had a clear view of Calthrop and Nat who were already a mile away. I clambered down the loose scree not caring now how much noise I made and checked that the horses hadn't been spotted They were still there. I unhooked my water bottle and took a swig, then slung it over my shoulder. In case. Exploring the place they'd been hiding in might take some time and I'd sweated a lot in the sun.

Then I re-entered the canyon through the pass. I moved Squawking Crow out of the sun into a hollow, and covered him with brushwood to hide him from the buzzards until I could get him back to his people who would look after him and give him a proper burial according to their rites and beliefs.

I crossed the dried-up water-course, traversed the rocky spur and climbed up to the mesquite grove.

I saw now that it covered the entrance to what looked like a natural cave, though I later found some traces suggesting it had been enlarged by mining operations at some point, though not recently.

I had already figured this out, but now I wanted to

test another thought: this must be a hidey-hole that Calthrop used to stash the proceeds of his plundering forays. Since he couldn't manage to transport the stuff without help, I also guessed Nat was in on it because he was useful. Probably he was the only one of Calthrop's men who knew the exact location of his cache. I didn't give much for Nat's chances of reaching three score years and ten.

Only two men knew about the treasure cave. Correction: three.

Inside, it was cool and shady after the bright heat of the sun. The walls were solid rock, and so was the roof except for a section which had been shored up by timber props. The cave seemed to go back far into the side of the mountain. The rocky roof dropped as I went but I was still able to walk without bending.

The further I got from the entrance the darker it became. In a niche in the wall a half-burned candle had been left. I lit it, walked on and then tripped and fell. A rope had been strung knee-high between the cave walls and I had not seen it in the gloom.

I was wondering why anyone would go to the trouble of setting a snare that had no point to it when I felt then heard a dull thud behind me. I got to my feet. It had grown very dark and I had to grope on the ground for the candle which had gone out when I dropped it. I made my way back to the mouth of the cave.

At first, I could not figure out why it wasn't getting lighter as I went. Nor could I explain the dust that had suddenly filled the tunnel. And then I knew what had happened.

The rope had sprung a trap made of ropes and geared pulleys which had pulled out whatever props had been supporting the timbers holding up the roof. That section was between me and the cave entrance.

I was trapped.

The dust made breathing difficult and I retreated. I decided to explore the rest of the cave until it had all settled. Then I'd be able to see and could start digging myself out.

I went back to the point where I had tripped and pressed on. After no more than about fifty paces, the cave became wider and higher, forming a vaulted chamber whose roof was too high for me to see. In the centre was Calthrop's booty. There were chests of different sizes. They contained coins, necklaces, silver snuff-boxes, ladies' brooches, gentlemen's tie-pins and such like, small items of large value and easily transported. Neatly stacked in makeshift racks against the wall were supplies and goods of all kinds, from nails and tools to city-made articles, sacks of flour, and bottles containing most things from patent medicines to branded liquor. These had been less easy to bring here but I guess Calthrop reckoned it was worth the effort. I couldn't have put a figure on what it was all worth, but it must have been a fortune.

No wonder Calthrop was prepared to bring the roof down rather than leave his ill-gotten plunder exposed to being spirited away. I reckoned the chances were small that anyone would ever notice the cave, let alone venture that far into it. But maybe Calthrop thought an Indian might, or a prospector, and he wasn't prepared to take any chances.

Around the walls were other niches in which candles had been placed. The one I had been using was burning low. So I gathered up three or four that still had a good life in them and made my way back towards the mouth of the cave.

The dust had cleared and I could see that the tunnel was blocked from floor to ceiling, completely filled by rubble like a cork in a bottle. I wondered how far the blockage extended. I thought hard and tried to get a picture in my mind's eye of the section with the props. I saw myself entering the cave, forced myself to recollect how far I'd gone, how many paces I had taken to pass by the props. I couldn't tell exactly, but it must have been around fifteen, maybe twenty. Just assuming that only the supported section of the roof had come down, it would take a dozen men with shovels a week to dig a way out. I was alone and I didn't have a shovel.

My prospects didn't look rosy.

I sat down on a rock and started to think.

Fact: Calthrop was ready to bury any over-inquisitive passer-by alive. That was no surprise. But burying intruders also meant burying his treasure, and that made less sense.

I took a small swig from my water bottle. Had to go

easy on the stuff. Might be here for some time.

Was Calthrop the sort who'd relish digging out twenty yards of rubble with only one man to help him? That didn't seem likely. That left two possibilities. Either Calthrop was prepared to sacrifice his plunder rather than let somebody else get his hands on it, or else he knew of another way into the cave. And if he could find it, then I sure could too.

While I was cogitating thus, my candle burned down. Before it went out I lit another. By its light I made my way back to the treasure room. As I went, I kept any eye open for any other glims that might have been left in niches along the way. I didn't know how long it would take to find a way out. But I did know that my chances of doing so would be greatly reduced if I had to work in the dark.

I found that the cave didn't end at Calthrop's dump but continued beyond it. It narrowed quickly and started rising as it went. Pretty soon I could no longer walk, however low I crouched, and had to crawl. This slowed my progress, but the tunnel didn't seem to get any smaller. The walls were less rocky too as though they had been smoothed by rushing water. I guessed that is how the cave had been formed in the first place.

From time to time I stopped to take a look at the flame of my candle. It continued to burn straight and upright. I'd been hoping to see it flicker. If it flickered, it would indicate a current of air, and air that moved had found a way in. And if it had found a way in, I could find a way out.

The further I crawled the hotter it got. It wasn't a good sign. I began to get thirsty. I took another pull at my canteen which was now considerably lighter. If the cave had been gouged out by water as I thought, there wasn't a drop to be had now, not even a suspicion of any dampness oozing through the cave sides. Soon I'd be sucking pebbles to stop my tongue sticking to the roof of my mouth. This was not good news.

I changed candles again and crawled on.

Then all of a sudden, the angle of the tunnel began to rise steeply and it got hotter still. Not only did my candle refuse to flicker, but I noticed the flame began to burn lower. I knew this happened in confined places where there was not enough good air to feed it. Soon I was finding it harder to breathe.

The air got so bad I wondered if I could go on. And then the problem was solved for me.

Without warning the tunnel came to an abrupt end. One moment I was painfully edging forward on my elbows. The next I was face to face with a solid wall of sheer stone. It looked as if at some time long ago, there had been a fall and a section of rock (and how big it might be I had no way of telling) had cut into the tunnel and strangled it. I had no choice but to shuffle back the way I had come.

It took some time before I reached a point where I could turn round.

I was by now pretty exhausted and rapidly running out of ideas.

Both on the way up the passage and on the way back, I had kept an eye open for anything resembling a fork or an opening in the walls or roof that might be worth exploring. But I'd seen nothing like that by the time I got back to the vaulted chamber.

My spirits had fallen almost as low as my water and my stock of candle-ends. If I didn't find a way out soon, I'd be reduced to looking for it in complete darkness.

I checked through Calthrop's loot to see if there was anything I could use, something to drink or eat, anything I could use as a tool. But in all the wealth he had heaped up in that cave, there was nothing of any practical value. There were plenty of bottles, but strong liquor and patent medicines were no use to me.

Rack after rack was filled with goods that had value only in the market place. I would have exchanged them all for a jug of cool water.

It was hard to reckon exactly how long I had been keeping company with all that wealth. A good few hours at any rate. The sun must have gone down long since, so it must be night outside. Maybe it would be dawn soon.

My candle end burned down. I lit another.

I made a tour of the chamber looking to build up my small store of glims. I had used up most of the ones that were in the obvious places already but I found sufficient replacements to keep me going for a good while. Some were only an inch or two long and good for half an hour or so. But others were three or four times that length, and all of them had smooth sides indicating they had burned down evenly, as you'd expect in a place where the air was still. All that is save one which I found standing on a box near a large crudely made press or cupboard made of rough planks with doors held by rope-hinges.

A column of tallow had formed on one side. I stared at it. And then I understood.

If tallow had dribbled down one side only, it was because the flame had pushed it in that direction. And if the flame had pushed it, it had not been burning straight. And if it hadn't been burning straight, there was a reason for it.

I opened the doors of the rickety press. Several others like it stood at irregular intervals around the cave walls. While the open shelves fixed by brackets to the rocky walls held candlesticks, mantel-clocks, silver teapots and other stuff of the sort, Calthrop had filled these cupboards with anything that might be damaged by any wildlife that came sniffing through the cave: rolls of cotton, linen goods, carpets, sacks of seed and meal.

I removed the contents and ran my fingers all round the interior. As far as I could see, it was what it looked like: a cupboard. But there had to be some reason to account for the candle with the grease that had run down one side.

The cupboard had been roughly knocked

together out of unplaned planks. They were thick and stout and very heavy and had been made into a rough box some six feet wide by eight tall and three deep.

There was no way I could move it even though it was now empty. I looked around and found a nail, a solid silver statuette, and a length of curtain cord. Standing on the smallest treasure chest, I used the statuette as a hammer to drive the nail into the top of the cupboard. To it I tied the curtain cord, which I used double for extra strength. Then I got down, heaved on my improvised rope and pulled her down. It wasn't child's play, but she gave in the end.

The fall raised more dust. As I waited for it to settle, I got my breath back.

The cloud cleared slowly, like a muddy pond when the dirty water is run off out of it by fresh. And that, if you say air for water, was what was happening. Most of the wall emerged as a uniform sandy-colour. But in the middle a large circular patch, maybe three feet in diameter, stayed black as though someone had painted a small solid cartwheel on it. The dust was being pulled into it. It was an opening, the opening to a tunnel!

I scrambled over the fallen cupboard and knelt at the entrance. The flame of my candle flickered.

I had found Calthrop's back door. It wasn't as wide as a church door but, if he ever had to use it, it would be plenty big enough to let all the goods he had stacked up in the cave pass through without trouble.

I reckoned the fact he had kept it deliberately hidden meant I was on to something.

I thrust the candle into the blackness which retreated before it.

I could see maybe four or five feet, enough to tell me the tunnel did not get any wider and led downwards. Holding my light before me I lay on my belly and crawled.

As I went I could feel the air cool on my face.

The tunnel levelled out after a while, dipped, levelled out again, widened and then came to an end in a sheer drop. I held my candle as far down as I could but couldn't see how deep the hole was. I picked a sizeable stone and dropped it. It hit something pretty quickly and then there was silence. I guessed what I'd heard was not a ricochet but the stone making a soft landing: it had not bounced. I guessed it had fallen into a mound of sand not too far below. I liked the idea better than a heap of sharp stones.

There was just enough room for me to turn round. This I managed with some difficulty. Then extinguishing my candle which would be of no use, for it would go out as I dropped and probably get jolted out of my hand when I landed, I slipped it into my pocket with the others, stretched my legs into the void and let go.

I couldn't have fallen more than eight or ten feet. Even so, my landing knocked the breath out of me.

Then I heard the sound of a match and saw a hand lighting a candle.

A voice said, 'Hold it there, mister! Don't move if you want to go on breathing!'

7

GOD'S FRESH AIR

A gun fired in church during the Sunday sermon wouldn't have given me a bigger shock than those words did.

'Who's there?' I said.

The sudden light made the surrounding gloom even blacker. The flame hovered about three feet above the sandy floor of the cave. It was perched on top of a short stub of candle that had been stuck with its own wax to a rock a yard high. It cast a small circle of light around it. Within that circle were a few loose stones. I made out a set of footprints among the stones. Nothing I saw moved.

'Toss your gun into the light so I can see it. Take your time. Do it slow. Don't make me nervous. When I get nervous, my trigger finger is liable to twitch.'

It was a strong voice. I couldn't place the accent, but it was from back East. I couldn't place the voice either. It reverberated in the enclosed space and seemed all around me. I narrowed my eyes but still couldn't make out any shape or movement. For no good reason I got the idea that whoever was there was alone.

'Hurry it up,' said the voice.

Then I thought this: how did I know he really had a gun? For all I could tell, he might be there in the dark pointing the stem of a corncob pipe at me.

Slowly I reached for my right hip. I took my gun out. Real slow, like the man said.

'That's better,' he said. 'Now just throw it into the light.'

'What'll you do if don't?' I said.

'Don't push me, mister. You can't see me but I can see you. I can blow your head off any time.'

I decided for the moment to hang on to my gun and see what happened.

'Listen,' I said. 'I could loose off a shot right now. I may not hit you but I'll see where you are in the flash. And my second shot won't miss.'

'I'm a reasonable man,' said the voice in an even tone. 'You tell me how you got here and why. I'll hear you out and then I'll decide if I'm going to kill you. I got time for it. Go ahead.'

Now, Pa had always learned me that talking was better than shooting. Added to that, I wasn't sure I could do what I said, I mean about bringing him down in two shots. Was I that fast? And though I had my doubts, I couldn't be certain he didn't have a gun after all. Anyway, what was he doing there alone in the dark? It didn't feel to me like he was there under his own willpower, as if he'd been passing by and had decided to spend the night under a roof rather than the stars. Our voices boomed like we were in an echoing chamber. Not a cave, then, but an enclosed place. It struck me it could be he was as trapped as I was. If that was so, then we needed each other. Four hands would be better than two.

'Your offer is pleasantly made, mister,' said I, though I kept the barrel of my Colt up in readiness.

I missed out the details and gave him the gist.

I told him how me and Squawking Crow had followed tracks into the canyon, how my friend had been shot by one of two men I knew—

'Name of?' said the voice.

I gave names.

'Calthrop,' I said, 'and Nat somebody.'

'Ames,' said the voice. 'Nathaniel Ames.'

Then I described how I'd found the cave, began to explore it, tripped the snare and brought the roof down and blocked the tunnel—

'You mean there's no way out?'

There was an edge of panic in the voice.

'Nope. Not that way.'

I heard the sound of boots shuffling across the sand. Then I saw them in the circle of light.

'Put your gun up,' said the voice. 'We got no quarrel with each other. We're in the same jam.'

A man appeared from my left and held out his hand.

My eyes were now accustomed to the dim light and I made out a tall figure, maybe in his late thirties, beard. He wasn't carrying a gun.

'Bridger's the name. Harry Bridger. And you?'

I told him my name, holstered my Colt and shook his hand.

'Now your turn,' I said. 'Who are you, Harry Bridger, and what in hell's name are you doing here?'

'Is that a canteen of water you have there? Anything in it? A man with a dry mouth ain't likely to tell a good story.'

'Let's see how you go, Harry. If I like what you got to say, you can have a couple of sips. Canteen's running pretty low. But I'm a reasonable man.'

'I got no more cause to like Calthrop and Ames than you have. But this ain't the place to go into all that. We got to find a way out of here. . . .'

'First tell me how you ended up in this place,' I said.

'Been tailing them for a couple of months. I got my reasons, but I'll save them for later. Last time was just a couple of days back. Saw them setting out from the Bar-T just before daybreak with a team of pack mules all loaded up. I guessed what it was: the loot they got from holding up banks and robbing honest folk, 'cos that's what Calthrop and his gang are up to these days. They drove the team out here, just him and Ames. But when they headed into the canyon I had to keep my distance for fear they'd spot me. By the time I followed them in, they'd clean disappeared. I reckoned there had to be another way out but I couldn't see it. So back out I went and rode round looking for it. I only found out for sure there was no such thing when I got back to the place I started from. Rode a complete circle. I was just in time to see them driving the mules back towards the Bar-T. By then the mules weren't carrying anything.'

'Here, Harry, you've earned your drink. But go easy on it, that's all there is. No telling when we might get some more.'

He took a couple of mouthfuls, handed the canteen back to me and went on.

'When they'd gone, I rode into the canyon and searched it pretty thoroughly. I didn't find anything and there was too much loose stone and shale to hold any marks a man could read tracks in. I couldn't figure it out. They brought loaded mules and they took them away unloaded. So where was the merchandise? I didn't hang around too long, since I had no guarantee they wouldn't be back. I returned next day. I made sure there was nobody about, did some more poking around and in the end I found the cave. I was still inside when they jumped me. Never heard them. Must have seen my horse. They had the drop on me before I knew it. Ames wanted to kill me then and there. But Calthrop was in one of his jokey moods. He puts a gun in my back and orders me to get into the tunnel you came through. Then he covered the entrance with something too heavy for me to move. . . .'

'. . . a cupboard full of loot. . . .'

'. . . and I been here ever since. Then you drop in and give me the fright of my life. Brad,' he said, 'we're in a jam.'

'You've had plenty time to look round. What have we got here?'

'I ain't rightly sure. It was a lucky thing I'd picked up a spare candle and still had it in my pocket, because Calthrop and Ames didn't even leave me a glim. But I had to be sparing with it. As far as I can make out, this chamber we're in now is a kind of dried-up siphon for some old water course that ain't had water in it for a couple of hundred years. It's just plain rock all the way round. So there's nothing doing down here. But then there's the tunnel you came in by, and just opposite, over there, there's another the same that leads on. I tried climbing up into it, but it's too high for one man. Couldn't get a foothold, the rock's too smooth. But now there's the two of us, I reckon between us we could get a man up there so he could find out where it goes. That way we might get somewhere. Anyroad, the way I see it, that's where we should start looking.'

I took heart from knowing I hadn't reached a dead-end. But Harry's plan wasn't as straightforward as it sounded. What if the man who was hoisted up decided not to give his hand to the one left behind?

And if he found a way out, what was to stop him just walking away and leaving the other one there?

'OK, Harry,' I said. 'But who's it to be? Me or you?'

He did not answer immediately and his hesitation told me that he had just thought what I had been thinking.

'Look, Brad,' he said, 'you're the one with the gun. If you hadn't fallen out of that tunnel and made me jump clean out of my skin, I'd have for sure died down here alone in the dark. I got no quarrel with you. We're in the same fix. We got to be pardners, like it or not. You're the lighter man. It makes sense for you to go. I'll trust you not to forget me.'

I held out my hand and he gave me his.

'Then it's a deal, pardner. Come on, let's get started.'

The distance from the floor of the chamber to the tunnel must have been about ten, twelve feet. I stood on Harry's cupped hands and clambered on to his shoulders. Above me the lip of the tunnel crumbled but eventually I found handholds and pulled myself up. I lit a candle and I was heartened to see the flame flicker again. I guessed the air current must flow directly from one tunnel opening to the next across the top of the siphon, for the flame burned upright down there. It was the same as those fast flowing streams which sometimes have fish feeding quietly underneath, in deep, still pools.

'What can you see?' asked Harry.

'The tunnel's like the one we came down. I got air

in my face. I'm going to see how far I can get.'

The way was level, then dipped, then straightened up. I passed a couple of larger chambers. There the air current was fainter. I guessed this was on account of the space being bigger, but each time I was afraid in case the tunnel stopped or would be too narrow for me to go on. But on I went. From time to time I shouted to Harry how I was doing. He replied. His voice got so faint until I couldn't make out what he was saying.

At last I reached a small chamber from which no tunnel led.

I turned over and lay on my back, fighting the fear and forcing myself to concentrate.

Fact: the trail had come to an end.

Question: if it was a dead end, why was my candle flame still sloping back the way I had come?

Answer: air was coming in all right, blowing the candle, but it was passing through spaces too small for a man to pass through.

Once upon a time, when it was a water course, the cave had been open. That was obvious. But since those days it had dried up and its mouth must have got clogged and sealed by falls of rock and rubble.

That was a likely explanation. But there was no way of telling how much rubble there was blocking it, no way of knowing how far I was at that moment from the sunshine. It could have been feet. It could have been yards.

I decided to go back and break the news to Harry.

Maybe he'd have an idea about what we could try next.

As I turned on to my stomach so I could start the long crawl back, I knocked the candle over. It went out.

I was plunged into darkness.

Almost.

As I reach for my matches, my eyes started to get used to the dark. To my amazement, I saw, to my right, just below the level of the roof, two, three small specks. At first, I thought they were some of those luminous gnats and flies you often get in caves and old mines. But as my eyes grew accustomed to the dark, I realised I was seeing daylight.

I relit the candle and held it up on that side. The flame bent away from it and then I knew I had found the source of the air current and our way out.

The cave wall there was formed of massed rubble. I pushed and poked it, but it was jammed tight. I managed to get a few pebbles out with my knife, but it was too solid to let me get any further.

That figured. If I was right and Calthrop had been prepared to block the cave because he knew he could always use this tunnel to get at his goods, then this was his back door. He'd want to make very sure no one would know it was there. He'd have seen to it that the tunnel was as tightly sealed as he could make it to hide it from straying Indians or curious prospectors. Still he wouldn't have plugged it so tight he could never use it if the need arose. But I didn't give a man lying on his side with the use just of his bare hands many chances of breaking through and getting out.

But maybe there was something in Calthrop's trove we could use for a tool.

It took me some time to get back to Harry.

I told him what I had found, the good news and the bad.

To my surprise, he laughed and thumped me on the back.

'Chin up, Brad. We're as good as home.'

If I'd known then what he told me later, that he'd been a prospector who knew all there was to know about mines, I'd have been less surprised.

'Now it's my turn to go a-roving,' he said. 'Give me a leg up. Not there,' he said, when I started to make for the side of the chamber with the tunnel I'd just been through, 'this one. I need a few things if I'm going to spring us from this trap.'

I hoisted him up to the tunnel that led back to Calthrop's treasure dump. I guessed he'd gone look-ing for something we could use as a pick.

He wasn't gone long.

When he got back he was holding a solid silver casket about six inches by four, a bottle of brandy and a length of cotton cloth.

He brushed away my questions and set down the items he had brought on the rock.

'Now to work,' he said. 'Give me your gunbelt. And this is what I want you to do. . . .'

By the light of the candle, following his instructions, I tore the cotton into narrow strips and plaited them loosely together until I had a length of about twenty feet.

Meanwhile, Harry took all the bullets from my gun and belt and was removing the gunpowder from them. In those days, a Colt used paper cartridges. So it took him no time at all to fill the casket.

'Trouble with powder is it just burns. It don't explode until it's fired in a confined space. Nearest thing I could find to a confined space for it was this handsome, tight-closing silver casket. Seems a shame to waste such a valuable article, but it's the best I can do.'

'What's the cotton and the booze for?' I asked.

'Fuse. I never pulled a stunt like this before. I hope it works. Let's go. I'll explain on the way.'

We wrapped everything we needed in what was left of the cotton cloth and tied the four corners together. Then I stood on his shoulder, hoisted the makeshift bag into the tunnel and climbed up after it. Then, with some difficulty, for Harry was a big man, I hauled him up after me and we started crawling along the tunnel.

When we got to the last chamber but one, I stopped while Harry went the rest of the way, to size up the job. He took my knife with him.

'I hope to God I got this right,' said Harry when he got back. 'Listen up and I'll tell you what's going to happen. I'll set the casket with the charge as far as I can into the section of wall with the air-holes. If I've used too much powder or not enough, we've had it either way. If the charge is too small, it won't shift the blockage and there's not enough gunpowder left to try again. If it's too large, it could bring the whole roof down and bury us alive. But whatever happens, there's going to be an almighty bang. You want to go back a stretch? Might be easier on your ears.'

'No, I'll stay with you. But I thought about the blast. I've got a candle left. There's enough wax in it to make earplugs for us both.'

'Good. I'll string the cotton along the tunnel and loop much as I can around the casket. When it's all doused in the brandy, it should generate enough heat to set the charge off. If not, I'll shoot it. A direct hit would do it all right. But I don't want to do that unless I have to. To shoot at it I'd have to see it, and if I can see it I'd take the full force of the blast. I'd rather be here out of the direct line in this cosy little chamber with you. Ready?'

Grabbing the casket and the brandy, he crawled into the tunnel, hooking the loosely plaited material to the roof as he went. On the way back, he soused the cotton with the brandy. Preceded by alcoholic fumes, he reappeared feet first and lit the improvised fuse. One on each side of the tunnel, we watched as it burned its way to the casket.

Once it seemed to go out and Harry was about to go in and relight it. But it caught again.

With ears full of candle-wax and mouth and

nostrils protected by what was left of the cotton, we cowered as close as we could get to the floor of the tunnel. I hoped most of the blast would go straight past us. But I knew we'd only get limited protection in the chamber were in.

Suddenly the silence was shattered by an almighty bang, the air was full of dust and my head felt as if ten men had sat on it.

But the roof had not fallen in.

Then Harry was shaking me by the arm.

I couldn't hear what he said for the ringing in my ears. I saw him mouth: 'Still there, pardner?'

I reached for the candle which had been blown out. I was still thinking of lighting it when I realized there was no need to.

I could already see Harry.

He had a broad grin on his face.

'Let's go!' he said

And we crawled over the rubble and out into God's fresh air.

8

STRIKING BACK

We didn't whoop none nor holler. We were both too bushed. But it sure felt good to be outside and see the clouds, breathe free and feel the sun on your face.

Harry's home-made charge had blown a neat hole in the slope about fifty feet below the entrance to Calthrop's cave and maybe some fifty to the left. This brought us out more or less on a level with the floor of the canyon and the course of the dried-up *arroyo*.

Our hearing returned and soon we could hear the wildlife singing and chittering and clicking again. I liked the sound better than the silence. Silence in such a place was scary.

Harry thought the same, though he said silence outside was nothing like as bad as silence inside a cave.

'I spent a lot of time in mines,' he said. 'Now a mine a man digs with his hands is a live thing. The walls drop stones, the roof drops dirt, and the earth you cut through goes on moving and shifting and settling long after you've moved on. You bring in timbers to shore up the ground over your head and they get squeezed and twisted and they sure let you know all about it. What with the falling dirt, the grinding of the rock above you, the groaning of the props as they take the strain, there's noise above, below and to both sides of you. The only time it goes quiet is when something's wrong and the tunnel you're in is about to cave in. When it goes quiet and all a man can hear is his own heart beating, that's the time to get out. Fast. A natural cave did all the settling it's ever going to do long ago. It's not alive: it's dead. That's why a man who's spent time in mines gets uneasy in caves. He feels that it ain't safe, that he got no business being there. Is that your friend?'

Abruptly changing the subject, he gestured to the pile of brushwood I had put over Squawking Crow.

'I must get him back to his people,' I said. 'That's what he'd have wanted.'

'Sure,' said Harry. 'But first things first. We'd better take us a looksee. We made a powerful noise back there. Might be nosy folks round about who could be friendly or maybe not so friendly, you never can tell.'

We picked our way cautiously through the pass and scoured the plain. We saw and heard nothing. We could have been the only humans on the planet.

Squawking Crow's horse and mine were where we

had left them, in the patch of mesquite, and his water-bottle was still slung round the animal's neck. He wouldn't need the water in it now. I shared it with Harry. Mounting the two ponies, we rode round the outside of the hidden canyon till we reached a pile of rocks. Beyond the rocks was Harry's camp.

While we rode, I told him my story, about how Calthrop had killed Bart and Eli in cold blood and how I wouldn't rest until I got justice.

Then Harry told me why he was all fired up about Calthrop. He'd gone out West for a prospector. He'd struck pay dirt but he'd been bounced off his claim by a fancy talker in a black suit and a red sateen waist-coat.

'Looks like there's a crowd of folks lining up to get him,' I said. 'The way things have turned out has made you and me allies. . . .'

At that moment a shot rang out, my hat was whipped off my head and I dived into a patch of prickly pear bushes.

I looked out and saw Harry, still on Squawking Crow's pony, laughing helplessly. In the end, he got his breath back and said I could come out.

'Don't fret. That was Rusty being friendly! Camp's behind those rocks.'

I said something about how some people have a twisted sense of humour; I recovered my hat.

'Lead on, Harry,' I said. 'Let's hope Rusty's got some tasty chow in the pot. I'm so hungry I could eat a mountain lion.'

We rode into Harry's camp.

I saw a covered wagon. There was a fire that made no smoke.

Then from back of the wagon, still carrying a gun, out stepped Rusty.

She was eighteen and her hair was flame-red. Turned out she was the daughter of Harry's partner in the Sacramento diggings, a man named McColl whom Calthrop had shot in the back. Harry had taken her under his wing, though she warn't no shrinking violet.

'Where'n tarnation you been, Harry?' she said. 'I was beginning to think Calthrop had got you.' Then she turned to me and said, 'Who's this?'

'Hold hard, Rusty, and stop pointing that gun at folks,' said Harry. 'Look, I ain't eaten for the last couple of days, nor drunk much, nor slept at all. I got a power of recuperating to do. Never saw a girl like you for asking questions. This here is Brad Chandler. Brad, meet Rusty McColl. And watch out, Brad, this one bites.'

'Nice to know you,' said I, holding out my hand.

'Mutual, I'm sure.'

She spoke the words as dainty as if we were in a Sunday parlour. But I could hear mockery in her voice.

'Well, if I'm not going to get anything out of you until you're fed and watered, you'd best sit yourselves down and eat.'

With upturned buckets for seats, we gathered

round the fire, each of us holding out a tin plate, and soon we were spooning up a mess of hard-tack, bacon and beans washed down with strong coffee that tasted as if it had been grown and brewed in heaven.

When we'd eaten our fill, we lit up and Harry told Rusty about how he'd found Calthrop's cave, how he'd been jumped and left to die and how we'd blown our way out.

'You know, Harry, that's just dandy,' said Rusty. 'It's a mighty fine tale for yarning round a camp-fire. But it don't get us no further forward than we were before. We've even gone backwards. Before, Calthrop didn't know we were on his tail. Now he knows and when he finds you're gone he'll be on his guard. By letting yourself get caught, you've lost the advantage of surprise. Same goes for Brad here. From now on, he'll be watching out for the pair of you.'

'Maybe,' I said. 'But before there's any more talk of going after Calthrop, I got to get Squawking Crow back to his people so they can give him a proper send-off to the Happy Hunting Grounds. I owe him that. He saved my life: I owe him.'

'Squawking Crow?' asked Rusty.

I told her how my Indian friend had taken care of me and how he had been killed. But most of my story of how I had vowed to get even with Calthrop for shooting Bart I left for another time.

I judged by the sun it was still some time off noon. That gave me plenty of time for what I had to do.

Harry said he'd come with me. But I said no. A white man bringing a dead brave back to camp can't rightly know for sure what sort of welcome he'll get. At least, Squawking Crow's people knew me.

So, leading the dead Indian's pony which Harry had used after we broke out of the cave, I got back on my horse and rode back to the canyon.

I sat for a while with Squawking Crow and made my peace with him.

Then I thought about what Rusty had said, how Calthrop would know the two of us were on his trail. The hole we had blown in the side of the hill was a giveaway. He'd know for sure we had both got out. But if the hole was stopped up, all he'd know is that Harry was still inside and that whoever tripped the rock fall was in there with him and just as dead. So I had to cover our tracks.

It took about an hour to block up the opening so it looked as undisturbed as it had been before.

I roped Squawking Crow onto his horse. This time I didn't try to hide my tracks but left plenty of signs to suggest that some of his tribe had taken him away. Then I headed out to where the Indians were camped.

As I approached, word spread like wildfire. Men, women and children lined my route to Kla Klitso's lodge. Before I got there, he came out to greet me.

By this time, the squaws were into their breast-beating and caterwauling and some of the braves looked mighty angry as if they thought their brother was dead on my account, which he was in a way.

I told Kla Klitso how Squawking Crow had died, how I had laid him face up so his spirit would be free to leave his body, how I had brought him to his people, and how I had sworn to avenge his death.

'Who did this thing?' said Kla Klitso.

I told him.

'I know this man. Bad man.'

And he told me again how bad Calthrop was. The world was full of people telling me how bad Calthrop was.

I said his enemy was my enemy.

He took this as a new sign of friendship and we smoked a pipe. When they saw this, the men of the tribe stopped watching and began to make preparations for the ceremonial burning of Squawking Crow's body.

I stayed a while, as courtesy required, but then left. A white man is out of place at such times.

I rode back to camp, got some much needed shut-eye, woke feeling refreshed, shaved for the first time in days and put away another helping of Rusty's chow.

While I ate, she told us what she had been up to while Harry and I had been catching up on our beauty sleep.

'A girl, not this girl at any rate,' she said, 'can't just sit around all day, just waiting and watching the clouds blow by. I thought I'd go take a look at this hidden canyon of yours. And you know what?'

She looked me in the eye.

'They've been back!'

'Who have?' Harry said.

'When I got to the defile that leads into the canyon, I saw tracks. A couple of riders had passed that way, and not long before. I hid my horse in the mesquite, like you did, climbed the slope and made my way along the side of the hill. From there, I saw two horses but no riders. Then I heard voices and Calthrop and Ames appeared suddenly out of the side of the hill. Something was worrying them. Ames looked down the slope away to his left. He shook his head. Calthrop said something back and shrugged his shoulders. Then they left. I gave them enough time to get a good start and came back here.'

'Don't sound like they spotted the back entrance had been blown,' I said.

Harry said, 'I guess we can take it Calthrop thinks we're still buried in that cave and don't suspect the pair of us are out and gunning for him. That buys us time. But time for what? What's our move to be?'

'The odds are against us,' I said. 'We got to shorten them in our favour.'

'Where'll you start?' asked Rusty.

'With old man Jebb. Runs the livery stables. He's a fair-minded sort and no admirer of Calthrop. If it hadn't been for him, I wouldn't have left town in one piece. He'll know as much as anybody about Calthrop and his set-up. He'll be only too pleased to help us any way he can. He might even know what happened to my pardners. I know Eli's dead. But last I heard Billy was recovering. Maybe the others stayed to tend him. If they're still around, they'll want to be counted in.'

As action plans went, this one wasn't as actionful as going in with six-guns blazing, but it was better than sitting around doing nothing. And Harry and Rusty relaxed now that something definite had been decided.

By this time the sun was going down and the light was draining slowly from the sky. That suited me fine. If I was going to ride into Berry's Crossing, I had to do it under cover of darkness. Calthrop had eyes everywhere and even after nightfall stepping on to his territory was like walking into the lion's den.

I checked my Colt and started out for town. Calthrop's town.

As I rode, I wondered if John and Pete were still hiding out like old man Jebb had told them to. Maybe they'd given up and gone home. Maybe they'd fallen foul of Calthrop. If so, they'd have been bested: horse-drovers are no match for professional gunslingers.

My thoughts were running on these lines when I heard the howl of coyotes. Seemed like there was a gang of them quarrelling just out of sight over a ridge way off to my left.

I'd come maybe three miles from Harry's camp. The sun was sinking fast now and the sky had changed from orange to crimson and was just starting to turn purple. It was that time between lights when a man sees things that aren't there ... and doesn't see things that are.

But it wasn't the light that made my horse nervous but the presence, just over the other side of that ridge, of more coyotes than was natural. I had pulled hard on the reins because my mount sure didn't want to go where I was telling him to.

As I crested the rise, I saw a hollow on the other side. There was something in it. It was as long as a man, but what looked like four spokes stuck out of it, so that the whole thing looked like a rimless wheel.

All around were the dark shapes of the coyotes which never stayed in the same place for more than a few seconds. My horse didn't like it. I could feel him trembling beneath me. I patted him on the neck and spoke quietly to him.

Then a voice said, 'That you, Rube?'

It sounded like sandpaper, as if it came out of a dry throat.

'Nat?' the voice said. 'I knew you wouldn't forget a pardner!'

I dismounted, keeping a hold of the reins, and walked into the hollow. The coyotes scattered but quickly regrouped and watched.

There was just enough light for me to make out a man spreadeagled on the ground. The moon picked out a glint of silver on his chest. But he didn't turn or move far. He couldn't. I saw why: he'd been staked out.

His arms and legs had been tied to wooden stakes which had been driven deeply into the hard ground. It was one way Indians executed their enemies. Sometimes they buried a man up to his neck, walked away and never came back. Other times they laid him out and pegged him flat on his back. Then they left him to the sun or the tender mercies of whatever wild creatures might come by. With his arms tied down, there was nothing he could do bar shout at them to scare them off. I once heard tell of a rattler that settled on a staked man's stomach, went to sleep, woke up and then slithered off again. But not before the guy had gone mad with fear.

'Now what do we have here,' I said.

'Who's there? C'mon, cut the goddamn ropes! You can't leave me here!'

'Don't see why not,' I said. 'As I recall, you weren't exactly charitably inclined last time we met.'

'What you talking about?' the voice croaked.

'I see you're still wearing your deputy star, Skate. Don't seem to have done you much good. Calthrop get sick of having you around?'

'Mister, I don't know who you are,' he whispered hoarsely, 'but you got to get me out of this. I been here almost a day. I can't take another.'

I had a full water-bottle. I unscrewed the top, held it over his mouth and poured. He drank greedily.

'You say you know me?' he said.

'Don't say you've forgotten, Skate. Two *bocarros* ride into town offering to sell old man Jebb thirty horses. You and Nat show up, take 'em off to the caboose and before the evening's out one of them's got himself kicked to death.'

'That warn't none of my doing, mister. I never had any part in that stuff. Sure, Rube made me his deputy and gave me a badge, but it was all a joke to him. He's crazy. When he was in the mood, he'd send me out and tell me arrest somebody. Anybody. Bring 'em back, he'd say, so I can have me some fun. This meant him being judge and jury and executioner. Nat went along with him because he and Nat go back a long way. But me, I couldn't stomach it. Before the killing started, they'd get good and drunk. They'd try to get me drunk too but I always acted like I'd passed out before they lost control. That way I never killed nobody and they never knew because afterwards they could never remember who'd done what.'

'So why didn't you walk out on him, Skate?'

'Because no one walks out on Reuben Calthrop. Are you going to cut these ropes?'

'Skate, Eli was killed and it was no accident.'

'I'll tell you what I know. Sure, I recall a couple of out-of-towners selling a bunch of nags to old Jebb. You was unlucky. Rube don't go wild that often. You rode into town on the wrong day, is all. Look, I'm sorry about your friend but I couldn't do jack spit to stop it. Are you going to leave me here to die?'

'Could be. I want to know how you suddenly got unpopular and ended up like this.'

'Who's asking?'

'Me. I'm asking the questions, Skate. I'm the one standing up and you're the one lying down.'

'All right. But if I tell you, you'll cut me loose? Deal?'

'Most like. Depends on what you say.'

'They thought I was dumb. But I ain't so dumb. This Calthrop ain't happy just sitting round town with a sheriff's badge on his lapel waiting for travellers, cowboys and *bocarros* to come by so's he can have him an hour of fun. He's a big operator. Got a ranch, thirty hands—'

'—And he robs banks and holds up trains. Skate, you're telling me things I know already. My rope-cutting knife's still in its sheath. If you want me to take it out, tell me something I didn't hear before.'

'And do you know why he pays thirty hands? Sure, some are cooks and house-boys. But most rustle cattle for him, tend them on the range, re-brand them and run them for sale as far as New Mexico. They get a share of the proceeds. Others, maybe a half-dozen, he takes with him when he goes raiding. They're all gunslingers and pretty hard men. When he gets back from a foray he gives each man his part of the loot. He don't stint with them. He knows better than to try and short-change men like that. But the biggest share always goes to him and Nat. But they don't keep their goods at the Bar-T, no sir. They don't trust them boys that hang around the place. So, they stash it some place else. I seen them. They send the hired hands into town to get drunk then load up

110

a couple or three burros and head out into the desert. When they get back, the burros aren't loaded no more.'

'So you reckon Rube and Nat bury it in the sand?'

'That's what I was trying to find out. Last night I saw them ride out, just before sun-up. Had their horses' hoofs muffled, and were acting cagey. I trailed them this far—'

'But they jumped you—'

'—then worked me over. Rube was out of control and wanted to beat me to a pulp but Nat told him no, said they had business, so why not just shoot me and be done with it. But that's not Rube's style. Too quick. So they staked me out and left me to linger. That's all I know, mister. So, if you'd oblige with that knife of yours. . . .'

'First tell me this. If you like playing dumb, how come you followed Calthrop and Nat? It was a risky thing to do. Anyway how come you're so curious about where they keep the goods?'

'And how come you know so much about Rube? And why are you acting so suspicious? Any rider passing by who finds a white man staked out would think he'd been left out for the coyotes by Indians. First thing he'd do would be to cut him free. Not you. You ask a lot of questions like I was a criminal and want the right answers before you'll lend a helping hand.'

'I know a lot about Rube because I want him behind bars. You know he killed Eli. But he also shot my brother.'

'Well, we're on the same side and want the same thing. I ain't Skate Skerritt. Name's Tom Earle, Sergeant, United States Army. Now cut me loose, you son of a gun, and I'll give you the rest of the story.'

9

PREPARATIONS

I cut Sergeant Earle free, sat him on my horse and, leaving the coyotes to bay to the moon, walked him back to camp.

While he got some of Rusty's chow inside him, he told the others what he'd told me and then we filled him in with our side of the story.

'So we all want the same thing,' said Tom, when we'd finished, 'which is to see Calthrop stopped. You've got your reasons. Well, so has the army. Friend Calthrop's been getting in the military's hair for a long time. First it was selling low-grade beef to provision the frontier forts. Then he started stealing payrolls carried by railroad and looting wagon trains and army depots, as well as making our job harder by riling the Indians in all sorts of ways and getting us blamed for all the bad things the white men did. But he's smart. Whenever we get close, he moves on.

However much the generals want to see him behind bars, they got nothing they can pin on him. That's where I come in. For the last six months, I been out of uniform, special investigator, working undercover, getting close to our man. My orders are to get the goods on him so the military courts can get him put away legal.'

'Save it for the jury,' said Rusty fiercely. 'We're going after him whether you're on board or not. And all this talking about it don't show how we're going to get the son of a gun.'

'Being an insider you'll have got to know more than we do about how Calthrop operates,' I said. 'But we got something you don't know: the place where he stashes his loot.'

I told him about the cave. He was impressed.

'It's what I needed. It links Calthrop to stolen goods. It's evidence no court in the land could fail to convict on. We've got him!'

'Now you tell us the rest of what you know.'

Turned out he wasn't as on his own in Berry's Crossing as I'd thought. Like me, he'd seen more to old man Jebb than met the eye. He'd backed his hunch and come clean, told him who he was and what he was doing in Berry's Crossing cosying up to Calthrop. Jebb shook his hand and asked what he could do to help nail the skunk.

Jebb kept his ear to the ground and used his livery men to carry messages for 'Skate' back to army head-quarters. The old man had told him Pete and John were still hiding up and looking after Billy who was on the mend.

'Where they at?' I asked.

'At first they holed up in a wreck of a barn old man Jebb used as extra stabling for his horses. They were safe enough there for a spell, but it was too close to the Bar-T for comfort. So they switched to an abandoned homestead on a hill the other side of town. Been there ever since.'

'Fine. I'll go bring them back here. We need all the guns we can get. There's three of us. . . .'

I caught Rusty's eye.

'. . . four of us. Another three wouldn't come amiss none. Meantime, we need you fit, Sergeant. So bed down and get some rest. You've had a busy day, but it's over. Mine ain't finished yet. I still got to go find my pardners. I'll be back around sun-up.'

The moon was higher and brighter than I'd have chosen for my purposes. The trail was straight and level and there was no real cover. Anything that moved would be visible from a long way off. I felt exposed.

But I had light enough to see something that brought me up short – a set of tracks left by a large group of riders coming from Berry's Crossing which forked off left in the general direction of the canyon where Calthrop had buried his plunder. Looked like the riders passed that way a good while before, maybe the previous day. And they hadn't come back. At least, they hadn't rejoined the trail that led to town.

I didn't know exactly what to make of it. But I had me half an idea.

About a mile before I got to Berry's Crossing, I swung left and followed the directions Tom Earle had given me.

Half an hour later, I made out a hill and, on the hill, a clapboard house.

The boys were as pleased to see me as I was to see them. But I cut the celebrations short and told the boys to pack up. I wanted us out of there before sun-up.

Billy was on the mend. Though his shoulder was still pretty sore, he helped load up all the provisions we could carry. We'd need them if we were to use Harry's camp as a base.

When we set off, it was still dark and the moon was down. We didn't see any early birds stirring and no one saw us. By the time we rode into camp, the sun had climbed high and was hot in the sky.

Harry had the place to himself. But it wasn't long before Tom and Rusty rode in. The sergeant had wanted to look the canyon over and Rusty had gone with him to show the way. When they got there. . . .

'You saw a gang of Calthrop's men, right?' I broke in.

'How do you know that?' said Rusty in surprise.

'Saw tracks headed that way. I guessed Calthrop would want the cave cleared. He'd have to bring his boys in to do the job.'

'There were maybe thirty, thirty-five of them,' said

Rusty, 'formed into a chain, passing out rocks and baskets of rubble which they tipped down the hill. They'd set up camp in the valley bottom.'

'Did you see Calthrop or Nat?'

'Sure,' said Tom. 'When we got there, they were directing operations. But they didn't stay long. We had a good view from the same spot as you were at, halfway up the hill above the defile.'

'Best seats in the house,' said Rusty with a grin. 'They should sell tickets.'

'Most of the cattlemen on the payroll were there,' Tom went on. 'I guess a few stayed behind at the Bar-T to look after the place and keep an eye on the herd. Calthrop was giving orders to Abe Chisolm. He's the Bar-T foreman. We were close enough for me to catch some of what he was saying. Told him he had to keep the men hard at it, but that they weren't to break through into the cave without him being there. He was most particular on that point. Said there were men with guns on the other side of the roof fall and Abe wouldn't want to mix it with them. Meantime, he and Nat had business to attend to. Said they'd be back in a couple of days. Then he and Nat lit out in a hurry.'

'If Calthrop's men get curious and clear that fall. . . .' I began.

'They've won't. They're gone,' said Tom.

'Decamped,' said Rusty.

'What d'you mean, gone?' said Harry.

'I couldn't let them stay there,' said Tom, 'and get

their hands on the loot. If they got in and found the stuff, they'd have split it up and cleared out. And it's our evidence, all we've got on Calthrop. I didn't want him flying the coop, not after all the weeks I've put in getting this close. So I left Rusty, slipped back out of the canyon, got on my horse and then rode in through the defile as if I'd galloped from town, making a noise and hollering for attention.

' "It's Skate," ' I yelled. I said a federal officer with a posse of thirty, forty sworn deputies had shown their faces just before sun-up. Sent by the governor upstate. They'd gone straight out to the Bar-T and locked up all the boys who'd stayed behind in the cookhouse and stood guard over them. They were holding them there until the judge arrived in town. A couple of the boys, Jimmy Toolan and Ephraim Perdue, had put up a fight. They were dead. The marshall had questioned everybody about the boss and Nat. He'd been expecting to find more hands at the Bar-T and asked where the rest were. Way things were going, he'd soon have an answer. I made out I'd managed to get away without being seen. I said I'd come to warn them to get out while they could.'

'You should have seen them scat! Dropped everything and ran for their horses,' said Rusty, and her eyes laughed at the memory.

'They fought with each other in the scramble to get out,' said Tom, 'and when they were through the defile they took off in whatever direction came first. When the canyon was quiet again, Rusty and me took a look at how far they'd got with the job.'

'They hadn't broken through,' said Rusty. 'No way of telling how much further needs to be cleared.'

'If they've gone for good—' Harry began.

'They won't be back,' said Tom.

'—then the odds have evened up a lot. There's almost as many of us now as there is of them.'

'Where'd Calthrop go?' I asked.

'He's gone on a job,' said Tom.

'What job?'

'There's a couple of army wagons headed out west from Independence, Missouri. It'll follow the Santa Fe trail as far as the Cimarron Cut then make south-west for Taos, its delivery point. On the way, it passes thirty miles north of Berry's Crossing. It'll be carrying a shipment of twenty-five thousand cash in silver dollars the United States Government has pledged to hand over to the Taos Indians in compensation for land transfers. No one's supposed to know about it. Somehow Calthrop sniffed it out. As well as Nat Ames, he's got six, no, seven hired guns. So as not to attract attention, the wagons will have only a small escort of ten or a dozen men. I tell you, Calthrop's boys will take them. They're good. It'll be just like drawing money out of a bank.'

'Twenty-five thousand,' said Harry. 'I never saw that much money together in one place!'

'It don't take up a lot of room,' said Tom. 'Stack it up and what you've got don't look much different from a couple of dozen boxes of cartridges.'

'Yeah, well, I'd like to see it before I die, that's all I got to say,' grinned Harry.

'And I sure would like to be there and put a spoke in Calthrop's wheel,' I said. 'But there's nothing we can do about it now. They got a head start and in any case we don't rightly know the place where they plan to ambush them wagons.'

'Won't matter none,' said Rusty, 'once we've got them lined up in the sights of a rifle.'

'Attagirl!' said Harry. 'That's fighting talk. Tain't ladylike. But it sure is fighting talk.'

'Yeah, but talk is all it is,' said Tom. 'It don't get us any further forward.'

Rusty coloured up almost as red as her hair, but she didn't say a thing.

'If it's action you want,' I said, 'I'll tell you what we'll do. Let's say Calthrop robs the wagon train. Once he's got the twenty-five thousand, he'll hightail it for the Bar-T so he can go to ground. But there'll a surprise waiting for him. By then word will have got around and the rest of the men will be long gone. When he finds nobody at the Bar-T, he'll come on out here to find out what's been happening from the range hands he thinks are still clearing the cave. By then, we've got to empty his loot out of the cave and find a safe place to stash it so he can't get his hands on any of it.'

'How're we going to do that?' asked Rusty. 'We don't have the manpower to clear us a way through the fall. Job's too big.'

'So we won't try it. We'll go in through the back door.'

'But I thought the tunnel was narrow,' she countered. 'You said you were crawling on your belly most of the time.'

'True. But nearly all the loot I saw was small items,' I said. 'Most of it was silverware, jewellery, coin, the sort of thing goes in bags or small chests that can be hauled and dragged. Whatever's too big to carry, we leave. But most of the stuff we can get out easy.'

'What would we do with it?' asked Harry.

I hadn't got that far with my plans. But here Rusty chipped in.

'There's another cave a little way up the valley,' she said. 'Found it when I was taking a look-see the day you got back here all tuckered out. It don't go back very far but it's big.'

'Rusty,' said Harry. 'You're a marvel!'

There were now seven of us: Rusty, Harry, me and Tom plus John, Pete and Billy Rively who said he'd make himself useful somehow. When we reached the canyon, I gave Rusty sentry duty. She took up a position high up on the hillside overlooking the plain. She was to let us know if she saw riders approaching.

We set to work clearing the mouth of the tunnel I'd blocked up. I posted Billy there so that if Rusty spotted trouble, she would sing out to him and he would call into the cave so we could get out. Then the rest of us crawled in one after the other. But we didn't all go the whole way. Harry took up a position on the outer side of the siphon. Then the four of us let ourselves down into it. Pete and John stayed put, while Tom and me climbed up the other side and crawled into the treasure chamber.

Tom and I ferried the merchandise as far as the inner lip of the siphon and handed it down to John and Pete who passed it up to Harry, who hauled the last stage of the way and handed it out to Billy.

After a couple of hours, I called a halt and we all came out for air, a drink and a smoke.

Rusty's cave was fifty, sixty yards further up the valley and well hidden. A large rock hid its mouth. We transported Calthrop's hoard and then wiped out our tracks. We re-sealed the tunnel making as sure as we could that only a pair of Indian eyes could have said that the way we left it didn't look natural.

By the time we were through, the shadows were lengthening once more.

'What now, Brad?' said Harry.

'Way I see it, Calthrop, Ames and any of the hired guns who've stayed with him will be here tomorrow, maybe tonight. So we got to be prepared.'

'That's right,' said Tom. 'We need to dig ourselves in, get us some cover.'

'Harry,' I said. 'You go scout out up there, where you'd have a line of fire on anyone entering or leaving the canyon. Build yourself defences to hide behind. You, Tom, take the grandstand view of the cave and do the same up there and make sure you've got cover.'

Harry took Billy and John, while Tom, Pete and me climbed the hill overlooking the defile and started building our hides.

It was now pretty late. We all had a bite to eat then tried to get some shut-eye: I had missed out on whole nights and was feeling bushed. We arranged a rota for sentry duty, so that we wouldn't be taken by surprise.

At first light, Rusty went out through the defile to check the horses and make sure they were good and hidden. When she'd tended to them, she came back into the canyon and went into the cave she'd found, and started organizing the supplies into two lots, one for Harry's team, one for mine.

She was still inside when Pete, who'd taken over the sentry watch gave a shout.

'Riders coming!'

I joined him on the shoulder of the spur. Their dust was clearly visible in the early morning light. They were maybe a mile off but coming fast. I made out half a dozen mounted men and a flatboard wagon. They'd be on us in minutes.

I called across to Harry and told him to hunker down.

Then Tom and me and Pete settled down behind the low stone wall we had built.

Below I heard the horses slow and then stop.

'You stay here with the wagon, Nat,' said a voice which I recognized as Calthrop's. 'The rest of you come with me.'

I peered through a firing hole to check on my view.

It figured. The defile was too narrow to let the wagon pass, so it had to stay outside. And if Calthrop's right-hand man was posted to guard it, then you could be pretty certain that it had the army's money on board.

My field of vision covered the entrance to both caves.

But I didn't pay it much attention, because out of the corner of my eye, I saw something move.

Rusty had just come out of her cave.

10

EAST TO THE BORDER

I couldn't warn her. It was too late: Calthrop and his boys were now directly beneath me.

But then I breathed again.

Rusty had heard them as they clattered single file through the boulders. Without waiting to find out more, she turned on her heel and disappeared back into the cave.

I turned my attention to Calthrop who dismounted and climbed up to the cave where his squad of range-hands should have been hauling rubble but weren't. His men stopped and watched him go. The canyon was so quiet you could hear the stones squeak under his boots.

He called out, but got no answer.

'Nobody at the Bar-T and nobody here neither,'

said one of his men, a tough-looking brawler, and he loosened the six-shooter in his holster.

'They run out on you, boss?' said another. 'What's going on?'

Calthrop stood at the entrance to the cave, pushed up his hat so it sat on the back of his head, and thought.

'Why were there men out here in the first place, clearing a fall in the roof of a cave? 'Tain't work for range hands. Don't make sense', said the brawler.

'Hold your talk, Shad,' snapped Calthrop. 'There's a lot at stake here. Come up. Take Shorty and go check inside. See if you can come up with anything. Nobody ever ran out on me before. Must be a reason for this.'

After a while, Shad and Shorty came back out into the sunlight.

'Nobody there. Don't look like there was a fight or any trouble. I'd say they threw down their tools and got out fast.'

'Don't matter a hill of beans,' said Calthrop. 'They're gone. Too bad for them, They brought it on themselves. The joke's sure on them!'

'Joke? What're you talking about, boss?' said Shad.

Calthrop got to his feet and called to the men who were watching events from the canyon floor, to come up.

'Boys,' he said, when they gathered at the cave mouth, 'it's time to move on. We done pretty good out of Berry's Crossing, but it's time to cut our losses.'

'What's this cave all about, boss?' asked Shorty. 'And why were cattle hands clearing it? Don't add up.'

'It adds up fine. I know you boys been grumbling about your cut. You've been comparing yours and mine and thinking mine's a lot bigger than yours. It's only natural. Well, I been keeping you on a tight rein on purpose. If I'd made your shares bigger, you wouldn't have had a reason for staying; you'd have run out on me. And by now you'd have spent every cent and be left with no more than a couple of dollars between you. Well, I been keeping a part of your cut back so that when the time came for us all to go our separate ways I could send you off with full saddle-bags.'

'You've been holding out on us!' said Shad, and there were murmurs of resentment from his companions.

'Sure I have,' said Calthrop, 'but it was for your own good. Just stop and think for a minute about the cowboys who've walked off the job. They've gone, so there'll be fewer to have shares, and because there's fewer to have shares the shares will be bigger. You get me? You'll all be rich!'

'Shares of what?' said a gunslinger in a red bandanna.

'The proceeds of the jobs we've pulled. It's all in the cave.'

The men looked impressed.

'Well, what are we waiting for,' said Shad. 'Let's

start clearing a way through.'

Calthrop again held up one hand.

'No need. There's a quicker way. Shorty, take a couple of men and get some lamps out of the cave. Shad, there's a box of dynamite inside. Go fetch a stick and then follow me.'

'I don't get it, boss,' said red bandanna. 'If there's a quick way in the back, how come you set the cowboys digging out the front?'

'I pulled them off the Bar-T because I wanted them here for when we got back from raiding the army wagons. I'd planned it to be our last job and I wanted to settle up accounts with all my boys. I sure didn't want them busting through before I got back because they wouldn't have waited. They'd have helped themselves and been gone long before we got back. Right?'

'I guess so,' said the man in the red bandanna.

Shad brought the dynamite and a length of fuse to where Calthrop was waiting outside the rear entrance to the cave which I had blocked up.

He stared at the spot and for a moment I thought he had seen through my handiwork. But he was only looking for the right spot to place the dynamite which he then rammed into a crack between the stones. He fixed the fuse, took cover, called out for his men to keep their heads down and struck a match.

The charge was too big for the job. It blew out the scree and exposed the tunnel all right. But it also blew out a chunk of tunnel above the mouth and left a large wedge of rock hanging over it. But a couple of men shored it up and made it safe. Then Calthrop told them what they had to do.

'Just think of it as gold-mining for dudes, boys,' he said with a smile. 'No question of breaking your backs digging out ore. Just bend down and pick up gems, silver, gold trinkets, whatever you can find that comes to hand, and haul it out. Now go to it. Get those lamps lit!'

Nat had come in through the defile to see what all the noise was about.

He and Calthrop talked together in low voices. I couldn't hear what they said. Then Nat took up a position at the mouth of the tunnel while the whole gang, with Calthrop leading the way, crawled inside. When they'd disappeared, he sat on a rock, reached into his waistcoat pocket, and rolled himself a smoke. After maybe fifteen, twenty minutes, he toiled up the hill to the cave, went inside and returned holding a length of rope in one hand and a stick of dynamite in the other. He fixed one end of the rope to the prop which shored up the rock hanging over the tunnel mouth, danced down the loose scree to the valley bottom, turned, dug his heels in the ground so he had good leverage and then pulled hard on the rope.

The area which had recently been blown out was unstable and with his second heave, it started moving.

He didn't need the dynamite.

He let go the rope and ran out of harm's way while a section of the hillside slid and covered the entrance to the tunnel.

It made no sense to me.

Unless, that is, Nat had decided he didn't need Calthrop any more. He had the army money loaded on the flatboard and was ready to go. If ever he wanted more, he could always come back and reopen the cave. That must be it: Calthrop had been double-crossed! Left to rot inside that hell-black cavern with the rest of his men!

And I and Harry and Tom Earle had been cheated out of our chance of getting our own justice for all the beatings and murders and mayhem he had committed!

But instead of turning away and making for the defile, Nat sat on another rock and rolled another smoke.

It was as if he was waiting for something.

He smoked his cigarette, threw the end away, and thought a while more.

What was he playing at?

And then I had my answer. My eye caught a movement, maybe fifty yards along the valley bottom, and then a flash of red hair, and Rusty appeared.

My first thought was that she'd got tired of hiding in her cave and, when everything went quiet and stayed quiet, she'd decided to come out and take a look.

I was wrong, for the next thing I see is Calthrop back of her, with a gun in his hand, pointing it at her and walking her down to where Nat was sitting.

I looked up and caught Tom's eye and cursed myself for a fool. I'd been so pleased with myself for finding Calthrop's back way out of his treasure cave that it had never crossed my mind that if there was one overflow tunnel, there might be others too.

The cave Rusty had found was fifty or sixty yards from the tunnel Harry and I had escaped from. That should have tipped me off: there was a whole network of tunnels. Calthrop had checked it out; why hadn't I?

And now I understood. He really had decided to move on. He didn't need his gunslingers any more. So he'd buried them alive. Quickest way of getting rid of them. He'd made sure he led the way into the cave. Once inside, he'd moved fast and got to his treasure chamber before any of them had even worked out how to get past the siphon. He must have got a shock to find the cupboard was bare. But he hadn't stayed there long worrying about it. He'd had to get out through the other tunnel before his men caught up with him. He must have thought it was Christmas when he came out into Rusty's cave and discovered not only her but his lost loot.

'What's this?' said Nat. 'Company?'

'Says she's alone,' said Calthrop. 'Reckons she was out riding, found her way into the canyon by accident, and then hid in the cave when she heard us coming.'

'What's your name, girl?'

'Rusty McColl,' she said, and, without hesitating, added, 'What's yours?'

'You by yourself?' said Nat, ignoring the question. 'If you were out riding, where's your horse?'

'What were you doing hiding in that cave?' asked Calthrop. 'What do you know about the stuff that's stored in there?'

Faced with a barrage of questions, Rusty folded her arms and looked her captors in the eye.

'I want answers,' said Calthrop, and without warning he hit her across the mouth with the back of his hand.

I had him in my sights. I guess Tom did too. But neither of us took the shot.

It wouldn't have been done in cold blood exactly. My blood was up, sure enough, but not enough for gunning even Calthrop down without him having a chance to defend himself.

But I did put a bullet next his foot.

He jumped as if he'd been holed and grabbed Rusty. Holding her in front of him, he gestured to Nat to stand close to him so he too could be shielded.

He looked up at where my shot had come from.

'Who's there?' he called.

'No friend of yours,' I said, and pulled the trigger again. A spurt of dust next to his left boot showed where the bullet had landed.

'Let the girl go,' I said. 'She's no part of this.'

'Listen, whoever you are, I'm walking out of here and she's coming with me. Try to stop me and she gets this.'

And he pressed the barrel of his gun against Rusty's right temple.

She tried to struggle, but he was too strong for her.

With Rusty as a human shield, and taking pot shots in our direction to make us keep our heads down, Calthrop and Nat picked their way carefully towards the boulders that marked the way out of the canyon.

I kept changing my position, but couldn't get a clear shot at either man.

Harry stood up from his position further back, but he, too, was unable to get them in his sights without putting Rusty at risk. Then all three disappeared into the defile.

All of us came out from behind our positions and, with me and Tom leading, scrambled around the shoulder of the hill, over the defile, and waited for them to come out the other side.

They didn't show.

Time passed like glue being poured from a jar. Then they came out in a rush, still holding Rusty in front of them but now backtracking as fast as they could go. And I still couldn't get a clean shot at them.

They'd gone twenty, thirty yards, almost all the way to the flatboard, when the entrance to the canyon erupted in a deafening explosion. I was knocked off my feet but not hurt. As I picked myself up, I remember the stick of dynamite Nat had not used.

I had lost my rifle in the commotion.

Rocks blown high in the air were still coming down. I saw Pete catch one on the head. He went down like a felled log. Tom was already out cold and there was no sign of the others in the great cloud of dust that was slow to settle.

I climbed the hill hoping to get a sighting of Calthrop over the top of the dustcloud. He and Nat had been too far from the blast to have been caught by it and they'd probably reached the flatboard without any trouble.

The dust thinned the higher I went until I had a clear view over the plain. There was the flatboard, going hell for leather already half a mile away, and Rusty was on board. They probably still thought she might still be useful as a hostage.

I scrambled back down to ground level and ran to the clump of mesquite where we'd left the horses.

The explosion had spooked them. One, caught in the head by a shard of flying rock, was dead. The rest had panicked, broken the branches they'd been tethered to, and were probably still running. But I was in luck.

Tom had tied his mount on the far side of a boulder. The rock had taken the force of the blast and his pony, a strong-looking piebald, was still there, trembling slightly but ready for action.

I patted him on the neck and said a few soothing words which helped quieten him. Then very slowly I unhitched him and, keeping a firm hold of the reins, swung up into the saddle.

By now the flatboard was out of sight. I reckoned Calthrop had a good ten minutes' start on me. But the wheel tracks showed up clear in the sand and soon I was rewarded by seeing a cloud of their dust in the distance.

I continued to gain on them but figured it would not be a smart move to get too close yet. I was outgunned and on a horse, a sitting target for whichever of them didn't have his hands full with the reins.

When I thought I was close enough, I dropped my speed and shadowed them. Sooner or later, they'd have to stop or they'd work the horses into the ground. Meantime, I knew they could see me, because I, too, was laying a trail of dust.

I had no plan except to keep my options open, which was no plan.

They kept heading east, away from Berry's Crossing. Calthrop was being as good as his word and was clearing out. I guessed he was heading for the border into Missouri. Different state. Different jurisdiction. The law couldn't touch him there for crimes committed in Kansas.

Under the great canopy of blue sky and scudding clouds, the plain stretched away endlessly. Here and there, the land rose and fell in shallow ripples. At intervals weathered sandstone bluffs reared up like great forts. Apart from them, there was nothing to break the monotony of the rolling plain. After a couple of hours, what I first took to be a blue haze slowly turned into a distant range of mountains.

Now that Calthrop had cleared out, I reckoned Tom would send Pete or John into town with a message to old man Jebb to get word of what had happened to Army headquarters. A detachment of troopers would be sent to tidy up the loose ends. Until they arrived, Tom and the boys would be more than a match for the gunslingers trapped in the cave. I guessed they'd leave them to fret inside until the fight had gone out of them, and then Harry, who knew most about burrowing through God's earth, would go in and lead them out, grateful to be alive and in no mood to put up a fight. Fine. But that didn't get me any further forward.

Of course, Tom would take off after me. The tracks of the flatboard and my horse were fresh and he'd have no trouble tagging along in my wake. But I'd traversed some stony terrain which didn't hold tracks like soft going. I didn't know how good a tracker Tom was. It didn't look good.

As I weighed up the situation, that sky got bigger and bigger and I felt smaller and smaller.

But at the same time, I felt riled as hell. Calthrop had Rusty. I'd only known her a couple of days but I felt somehow responsible for her. I knew she could look after herself in most of the fixes folk get themselves into, but with a man like Calthrop, you never knew what he might do next. I figured she needed help and there was only me now to give it.

The trail of dust thrown up by the flatboard thinned. I stirred my horse to a canter and then, as the cloud faded altogether, to a gallop. Without their dust, I couldn't make out where they were at.

Maybe they'd hit a stretch of gravel and weren't throwing any up. But maybe they'd stopped. Maybe they'd hit a rock or found water. Maybe they had a good reason for stopping. But maybe the reason wasn't good.

Suddenly I had a real bad feeling.

11

DESTINY TRAIL

The going now became more broken but also greener. The country wasn't open any more. It was a landscape made for snipers, surprises and ambushes.

By now I'd lost the trail of the flatboard and, hoping to get a sight of it, I climbed a rocky knoll. Reaching the top, I lay flat on my belly and looked over the edge. Below me was a trail which I would have crossed in another half mile if I hadn't stopped. It ran left to right, curved round a fold in the land and then I couldn't see where it went after that. But something moved on the road just before it got cut off: a covered wagon bowling along smartly.

I stood up. It was peaceful and deserted. Then I heard a horse snicker.

The sound came from a clump of trees which hid a section of the road directly below me. I looked round again, saw nothing suspicious and reckoned the coast was clear. I led my horse down the slope, tethered him to a branch and covered the last hundred yards at a crouching run.

I needn't have taken the trouble. The two men were good and dead.

They were lying in their own blood on the verge. One had a hole in his head and the other in his back. Just yards away the army flatboard stood in the shade of the trees. The two horses that had hauled it were happy enough to be taking it easy. They'd found a patch of tasty green grass and were nibbling at it contentedly. There was nobody around except the dead men and there weren't any boxes of silver dollars on the back of the flatboard.

A man didn't need a giant brain to work out what had happened. John Doe and Joe Hick had been jumped and their rig had been stolen. Nor was it hard to guess who'd done the jumping: Calthrop and Nat had switched wagons. They, Rusty and the money were still ahead of me.

I hitched my horse to the back of the flatboard, got into the driving seat and headed off in the direction the wagon had taken. I didn't need to go fast and this way I'd rest Tom's pony. Having a rested mount might be useful later on.

Now and then from a rise on the road I got a sight of the wagon up ahead, still moving along at the same pace. It didn't look like Calthrop and Nat were taking the trouble to check if they were being followed. I guessed they figured they'd got clean away.

By now, the shadows were getting long and I started to worry. How would I keep on their tail once it got dark? As I crested a gentle hill, I stopped and peered into the gathering dusk. The road ran on white and straight for a couple of miles.

There was no wagon on it.

But about a mile along, a track turned off to the left. Someone had planted trees along it. For the shade, I supposed. As I watched, I saw a patch of white move between the branches: it was the covered wagon I was chasing.

My eye followed the line of trees and found a huddle of one-storey buildings: barns and stables and the like. A chimney was visible atop one of them, but no smoke. I couldn't see any animals either nor hear any of the usual farmyard activity. It was a homestead. But nobody was home.

I watched the wagon drive into the yard and stop.

Two men got down and checked the outbuildings. When they were satisfied nobody was about, they returned to the wagon and dragged a third figure from beneath the wagon's canopy. I saw a flash of red hair. Then they went inside.

Smoke appeared at the chimney. One of the men came out and wandered into the trees. I heard a shot and saw him come back holding whatever he'd shot, a jack-rabbit, maybe a hare. Then he went inside again.

By now it was dark enough for me to get closer. I drove the last mile and left the flatboard at the start of the tree-lined branch-off that led to the farm. Although there'd be a moon later, the shadows just now were dense and black. I walked the length of the track and reached the homestead. There was a light in one window.

I entered the yard. Keeping close to the wall, I worked my way slowly to the lighted window. The glass was misty with dirt. One pane was missing. I peered in.

Calthrop and Nat were sitting at a table eating the jack-rabbit they'd roasted on the fire which was now dying back. There was no sign of Rusty.

'Should get to the border late tomorrow,' said Calthrop between mouthfuls.

'Like I said, I know a place where we can cross the river without attracting attention,' said Nat. 'Somebody there owes me a favour.'

'Then it'll be easy street.'

'What about the girl?' asked Nat.

'We'll keep her till we get to your friend, the one who owes you the favour. She could be useful if we get in a jam. But once we're crossing that sweet river, we'll see if she can swim with a rock tied to her feet.'

'Pass the bottle,' said Nat. 'I got a thirst on me.'

Calthrop passed the bottle, but not before taking a long swig from it.

I left them to it and worked my way further round the house. I passed several windows, all dark, before coming to one from which there came a faint glimmer.

141

Slowly I slid right up to the edge of the frame, looked in with one eye. By the light of a candle I saw Rusty, bound hands and foot, stretched out on a truckle bed.

I guess I could have gone back and taken Calthrop and Nat right then. But before there was any shooting I wanted Rusty out of that place and away from danger.

I tapped lightly on the window pane. Rusty took no notice. Maybe she was asleep.

I tapped again.

This time she stirred and looked straight at me.

I held one finger to my lips, but she had too much sense not to know she should keep quiet or else we'd have Calthrop and Nat walking in on what should be a private party.

I eased the casement open, stepped across the sill, and cut the ropes that held her.

Without saying a word, she rubbed her wrists and ankles to restore the circulation. Then she was ready to go.

We skipped out the window, felt our way along the wall as far as the yard gate and were about to head down the tree-lined track back to the flatboard, when the house door opened and a patch of light spread across the yard.

'I'll do it,' said Nat. 'I won't stable them, though. I'm too bushed. But they ought to have a feed if they're going to pull the wagon for us all that way to the Missouri tomorrow. And while I'm about it, I'll get another bottle from the wagon.'

We froze in the shadow of the wall while Nat opened a couple of barn doors before finding some hay and a pitchfork. It took him about ten minutes to feed the horses. He got a bottle from the back of the wagon, then went back in the house and shut the door.

We moved out of the yard and when we were under the trees and it was safe to talk, I told Rusty about how I'd followed her. I also explained the plan I'd thought up while I'd been waiting for Nat to finish his chore with the horses. I thought she'd say I'd be a fool to risk it. Instead, she said she'd help: with two, it would be quicker.

What I'd thought was this. Why should Calthrop and Nat get to keep $25,000 that didn't belong to them? Like Harry, I'd never seen that amount of money in one place, but I recalled what Tom had said and pictured it looking more like a small hillock than a mountain. Mountains are hard to shift, but it don't take giants to move hillocks.

We went back to the stolen rig. I climbed over the duckboard. Inside it was blacker than the back of a grate. I felt around with my hands and located clothes, a coil of rope and a wicker-covered gallon jug which was about three-quarters full, I hoped, of water. I pulled the cork and sniffed: it did. I took a pull, for I was dry. I fumbled around some more until I found a wooden box, something the size of a cartridge box. I located another, then a third, until I counted twenty-five. Each had a handle on top for carrying. I lifted one. It was lighter than I thought it would be. I'd have thought a thousand bucks in silver dollars would have weighed more.

There was no way we could move the wagon without attracting attention. We'd have to manhandle the boxes back to the flatboard.

I passed out the first to Rusty who took it and set it on the ground. Then I got a second and lifted that out too until in the end, all the boxes were all lined neatly in a row, like soldiers.

I picked up one in each hand and started back towards the flatboard which was 2 to 300 yards down the tree-lined track. Rusty got hold of a box and followed. The first three we stashed on the back of the army flatboard which then I backed up the track maybe a couple of hundred yards. This made some noise but we were too far from the house for it too matter. Then we loaded the rest of the boxes. At the last minute, I remembered the water-jug.

All this took some time.

Before we got away, I went back to the rig, unhitched the horses, tied them with Tom's pony to the back of the flatboard which I walked back to the road, making as little noise as possible. When we got there, I jumped aboard and took us out of there. After a mile, we disappeared over the rise from which I'd first seen the branch-off to the homestead. I knew we'd made it. I gave the horses their head.

The moon was well up and we made good

progress. I aimed to put as many miles between us and them as I could before they woke up and figured out what had happened and decided what to do about it. I didn't underestimate them. The first thing they'd do would be to get hold of something to ride. Rusty said she'd heard horses nearby, maybe in a neighbour's field. It was safest to assume she was right. I reckoned we had at most a six-hour start.

Joe Hick and John Doe were still lying on the grassy verge where they'd been shot. I'd been hoping they'd been found and that there'd be law waiting to question anybody riding by. We could have done with some help. But there was only us on the road.

The moon was high enough for me to recognize the knoll from which I'd first seen the road. I turned off it and headed back towards Berry's Crossing the way I'd come.

The horses which had pulled the flatboard from the canyon were tiring badly. I stopped, turned them loose and switched to the ponies from the rig Calthrop had stolen. Then we went on our way again.

The sun came up and we were raising up plenty of dust. We were leaving trail as easy to see as the Milky Way on a starry night. From time to time I checked back of us. I didn't see any riders coming after us.

We were now reaching terrain where tall bluffs rose out of the flat plain. The flatboard began to bounce around, for the trail here was uneven. I dropped our speed but even so we still hit a rock hidden just under the surface. Not too hard, but hard enough to break the front axle. The flatboard didn't turn over and Rusty and me got off with a no worse than a bad shaking. But both rig ponies broke legs and I had to shoot them. That left us in the middle of nowhere with $25,000, no food or water and just one horse – Tom's pony – between us.

I looked around. Behind us, still no sign of Calthrop's dust. Ahead, the plain rolled away until it merged with the sky. To our right stood a towering sandstone bluff with a litter of great boulders around its foot.

'Listen, Rusty, we got a choice. We can get on Tom's horse and get out of here. We've got a good start on Calthrop and half a chance of making it if we go now. But he and Nat will follow our trail and find the flatboard for sure, and the money. . . .'

'I wouldn't want that,' said Rusty. 'Not after all the killing he'd done to get it.'

'Then we move the money, bury it under the bluff yonder. If we do it fast, we might still get out while we've still got an edge.'

I didn't care to think what would happen if we didn't keep that edge.

It took us more than an hour to hide the twenty-five boxes among the boulders at the foot of the bluff that towered high above us. We put them in a shallow hole we scooped out and covered them with sand. It was thirsty work and without the water from the wicker-covered jug it would have gone hard with us.

We were all set to ride out of there on Tom's horse

when Rusty suddenly gave a shout and pointed back the way we'd come. In the distance was a cloud of dust thrown up by a party heading in our direction. It had to be Calthrop and Nat. They'd picked up our trail. We had no choice but go to ground. With two of us on one horse, they'd soon run us down.

I fetched Tom's pony and tethered him out of sight among the rocks. Here we had some cover, but we'd be exposed if they got round our flank. I looked for a way up the bluff. I didn't like the idea much, since it would mean leaving us without an escape route. But it was all we had.

The rock was badly weathered. At times it crumbled under hand or foot, but there were also firmer horizontal ledges, vertical funnels and even small platforms where we could stop and watch what was going on below without being seen. I left Rusty on one of these while I tried to go higher. I wanted somewhere less accessible. It took me some time to climb another thirty feet, but I was rewarded by finding a wide ledge directly above the platform where Rusty was keeping watch. I leaned over to tell her how to get up and join me, but she shushed me and pointed down. What I saw made me duck my head.

Calthrop and Nat had almost reached the flatboard. They dismounted and hitched their horses to it. One glance was enough to tell them it was full of nothing. No runaways, no boxes full of army money. Suddenly they both stiffened. I'd heard it too.

Tom's horse had snorted.

Realizing they made a plumb target, they took cover behind the flatboard. I guessed by now their guns were out and they were looking for something to shoot at.

They stayed where they were for five, ten minutes. When nothing happened, they reached out carefully and unhitched their horses, then keeping the ponies between them and the boulders as a shield, they moved slowly towards the bluff. Then they were cut off by the overhang and I lost them. But if I couldn't see them, I could hear them. They searched the rocks. First they found Tom's horse, then our tracks.

Though they talked in whispers, the sound carried and I caught enough here and there to have an idea of what they were doing. Calthrop ordered Nat to climb the bluff after us while he stayed on the ground in case it was a trick and we suddenly broke cover and took off on their horses.

I poked my head over the edge and tossed a pebble to get Rusty's attention. When she looked up, I made signs for her to climb up to where I was. Nat would be up on her quickly. I crept back the way I'd come up, thinking to meet her and hand her up the tricky part of the climb. But I was too late. Negotiating a shoulder of rock, I glanced down and my blood froze.

Rusty stood at the bottom of the ten-foot tall funnel or chimney which I'd climbed with some difficulty. Behind her I saw Nat's head then his shoulders then the rest of him, including the gun which

148

appeared in his hand. He grabbed her by the hair.

'Rube, I got the girl!' he shouted.

'Bring her down!' Calthrop shouted back. 'We'll get some answers out of her!'

By this time, I had my Colt out. But I didn't have a clear shot. I put my gun up and slid down the funnel. Nat headed back down the way he had come up, still holding Rusty with his free hand. She was kicking and screaming and that slowed him down enough for me to gain a few valuable yards on them.

I wasn't trying to be quiet any more. Nat heard me coming, slammed Rusty against the rock wall and turned. She looked dazed but took her chance. She shuffled along the ledge out of his reach and dodged out of sight round the next corner. Nat let her go and got in one shot at me. I heard the slug scream past my left ear. Then I was on him.

Nat was a big guy. But I'd been waiting for this moment a long time and my dander was up. My momentum drove him back against the wall. I heard him gasp and the shock spilled the gun out of his hand and sent it slithering over the edge and into space. I pushed myself back off him and caught him high on the temple with a left. He rode it and, recovering fast, came back at me with a haymaking right which would have taken my head off if it had connected. But I got my chin out of the way in time. The force of his follow-through made him lose his balance and as he stumbled past me, trying to regain his footing, I hit him behind the left ear. He went down on all fours but took it better than I thought, because I'd caught him square with a good punch. He shook his head, half raised himself and, as I closed in, he tucked his head between his shoulders, threw his arms around my knees, pulled me down and threw himself on top of me.

Like I said, he was a big guy and his weight prevented me breaking his hold. He pinned me by the arms, leaned back and for an instant we stared at each other. I saw in his eyes that he recognized me. He knew why I was there and that only one of us would leave that place alive.

A picture suddenly came into my mind of Eli's twisted body on the floor of Sheriff Calthrop's office and I got even madder than I was before. I shoved him off me and was on my feet before he got up. He lunged at me. I sank a big right into his waistcoat and heard the wind whistle out of him. His head dropped but I straightened him up with an uppercut that caught him clean on the chin. The punch had all my weight behind it. I don't think he knew what hit him. But he didn't go down straight away. He staggered back with his arms flailing. Then he was off balance and suddenly he was gone. I peered over the ledge. He was spread-eagled on the ground below, staring up, not moving, one hand within six inches of the gun he had lost in the fight, and with his head lying at an unnatural angle. One glance was enough to tell me he was dead. One glance was all I could spare him. I had to find Rusty before Calthrop got hold of her. But looking over the edge, I saw Rusty being frog-marched at the point of his rifle. I reached for my Colt but before I could get a shot in they disappeared into the rocks.

But if I couldn't see Calthrop, he'd seen me. There was the sudden crack of a rifle. A large lump was blown out of the sandstone wall just next to my head and my hair was suddenly full of gravel. I ducked out of sight before he could fire again.

'Time to parley, friend,' he called.

'I'm no friend of yours,' I replied.

'What are you, then? The law?'

'I'm your past catching up on you, Calthrop. Let me jog your memory. I'll give you a few names. Do you remember Harry Bridger? No? Or Eli Hook? Then how about Bart Chandler?'

'What's this, guessing games? I got no time for this.'

'I'll give you the answers. Harry Bridger owned one of the claims you jumped over Sacramento way. There's a lot of men out there you robbed who'd give a lot to have you in their sights. Eli was a *bocarro*, a friend of mine. You kicked him to death in Berry's Crossing and you'd have done the same to me if I hadn't got away. It was the night you had the back of your jail pulled off. . . .'

'I know you now,' said Calthrop. 'Pity I didn't finish the job when I had the chance. It would've saved me the trouble of doing it now.'

'Brad Chandler's the name,' I went on. 'Bart was

151

my brother. About two years back you shot him because he beat you fair in a horse race.'

'Could be,' said Calthrop, with a sneer in his voice. 'I never was a good loser.'

'But you've got out of the habit of winning lately. First you lose the Bar-T, then loot you stashed in the cave grows legs and walks, the army money you stole vanishes into thin air, and now Nat's had an accident. . . .'

I heard him snarl and I smiled. Now he really knew who I was. Now he knew why he was soon going to pay. But it wasn't over yet.

'I want that money. I know it's here,' he said. 'You got a choice. You can tell me, or I can beat it out of the girl.'

I backtracked fifteen, twenty yards along the ledge, stopped and risked a glance down. Even with the change of angle I still couldn't see him. It looked as if I was going to have to go down and get him.

I went down.

On the way I weighed the odds. Calthrop wouldn't kill both of us. If he did, he'd never get the money. I reckoned he wouldn't want the girl dead: she was a lever he could use against me. He'd threaten her to bring me out into the open where he could gun me down. With me eliminated, he'd be free to make her talk. And when she'd talked, she wouldn't be useful any more. . . .

I heard a sound that could have been a slap or a punch and Rusty cried out in pain.

'Are you getting my point, Brad?' Calthrop called.

'Looks like you got all the high cards,' I replied. 'Let the girl go and I'll show you where the money is buried.'

'No. You throw your gun down where I can see it and come out with your hands in the air. Them's my terms. Do as I say and the girl won't be harmed.'

'You got me square,' I said, and I tossed out my gun and stepped out of the shadow into the sun.

Rusty appeared round the rock that had been shielding her and Calthrop. There was an angry welt on one side of her face. She jerked up straight like you do when someone jabs the barrel of a rifle into your back.

'Show me where you put the goods,' said Calthrop.

I thought a moment, then said, 'This way.'

I led, with Rusty and Calthrop following in that order. If Rusty was surprised I was going in the wrong direction, she didn't show it.

I glanced over my shoulder. Calthrop was getting excited, jabbing Rusty to make her move faster, peering round her to get a better view of where we were going.

We were going towards Nat who was still staring up at the blue, blue sky. When I was within a yard of him, I paused.

'Why're you stopping?' barked Calthrop.

'Nat's eyes. They're still open. A dead man's eyes ought to be shut. You want me to do it?'

'Leave him. It don't make no difference to him now. Nor to me neither.'

'Respect for the dead,' I said and bent down. Calthrop put a bullet into the ground next to my foot. I used the commotion to roll over Nat and scoop up the gun that had spilled out of his fist when I'd slammed him against the rock high above. His second shot went wide, for Rusty dug one elbow into his midriff and spoiled his aim. By then I was on my feet. As I turned, I got off a shot that caught him in the shoulder and spun him round.

Rusty grabbed his rifle off him. But he recovered quickly. With his good hand, he reached for the pearl-handled six-shooter in its fancy holster and loosed off a shot. I felt a searing pain in my calf which almost took me down as I fired.

Calthrop threw up his arms, dropped his gun, staggered back three or four paces until he was stopped by a boulder. He stood there for a moment, a deeper patch of crimson showing against the red of his waistcoat, and then slid down the rock until he reached a sitting position. It was the last movement he ever made.

Rusty turned to me and said, 'If Harry was here now, I know what he'd say.'

'What?'

'Attaboy!' she replied, and she threw back her head and laughed.

12

THE HOMECOMING

Calthrop's bullet had passed clean through my right calf. It wasn't a bad wound but it bled a lot. Rusty took the lace from my boot and used it as a tourniquet. After a while, the bleeding stopped. But when we tried getting me on one of the horses Calthrop and Nat had trailed us on, it started again. She tied it tighter, so tight I almost passed out.

We left the bluff as we'd found it, except for two dead bodies and twenty-five boxes of US dollars hidden in the sand. Someone else could bury the dead and unbury the money. We'd send men back to do it. It was army money, so the army could look after it. But we were through. All we wanted now was to be somewhere friendly, with people who didn't point guns at us.

I figured we were still a six–seven hour ride from Berry's Crossing. There was plenty of the day left and ordinarily we'd have made it easily by nightfall. But ordinarily didn't come into it. I had to take it slow and as the day wore on and we finished the last water in the jug I started to worry. By now I had a fever and was burning up with thirst.

When it got dark, Rusty said we should stop and rest until the moon came up. I laid my head down on my hat for a pillow and must have dozed. For the next thing I knew, Rusty was shaking me by the arm.

'There's something going on, Brad,' she whispered. 'I can hear calls from birds that don't call at night. It's got to be Indians!'

I sat up and listened. My ears were filled with the noise of blood pumping round my body. But over it I heard the cry of a whippoor-will. I cupped my hands and answered. The next moment four shapes emerged from nowhere and stood before us.

Rusty gave a shriek.

'Bringer-of-Fire sick again,' one of them said.

Beams from the rising moon glinted dully on his necklace of spent copper bullets. It was Kla Klitso leading a night hunt.

'Sick in leg, old friend,' I said, and I smiled.

'Who do this thing?' he asked

'The one you call *millahanska*, "White-man-with-silver-shining", great enemy of the Kepwejo. But he's stopped shining. Dead men don't shine.'

Kla Klitso thought a moment then he managed a smile.

From then on, the going was smooth and I can

wrap up the rest of the story quickly.

The Indians gave us food and water. They tended my leg and escorted us back to Berry's Crossing where we met up with Tom, Harry and the rest of the boys.

As I thought, Harry had left Calthrop's gunslingers to cool their heels in the cave before going in and bringing them out. They were no trouble. He handed them over to the platoon of soldiers the military had sent in response to the message Tom had passed through old man Jebb.

A detail was sent out to the bluff. The bodies of Calthrop and Nat were brought back for identification and burial, and the twenty-five boxes continued their way to Taos.

My leg mended and I started thinking it was time I went back to my folks in Colorado. By then, most of the cattle, money and other goods Calthrop had stolen or looted had been recovered and a percentage was set aside as a reward for those of us who'd brought his reign of terror to an end. I had more than enough money to pack up and go home.

One day, Pete and John said they were ready to go too. Even Billy was homesick for Cedar Bluff, for all that his wife would be waiting for him. Tom had to report to headquarters where he'd get a new posting. Harry wasn't sure what he'd do. He found it hard to get used to the idea that he'd made more money catching villains than by doing the only thing he believed he was good at, looking for gold. He hated the thought of going back to Tamblin, Ohio, his home town, where he'd die of respectability. Instead, he reckoned there might be gold in the Colorado hills and was minded to try his hand prospecting them. As for me, I was ready and anxious to go back with the bagful of money we Chandlers would need to defend our interests.

And Rusty? Well, we'd come to what genteel folks call an understanding.

So it was decided we'd all travel together.

Still a farm boy at heart, I hoped I'd seen the last of greed and fighting and bullets. But I never could bring myself to hang up my gun.

A man sooner or later learns it is a sensible thing to put the past behind him and turn his face to the future. But it's also worth bearing in mind that the truly wise man don't forget easy and always keeps his gun well-oiled and hanging on the peg next his hat.

Just in case.